Life, Love, and the Pursuit of Hotties

Katie Maxwell

SMOOCH NEW YORK CITY

This book is for all of Emily's readers who took the time to write me and ask for more Em books. I greatly appreciate all the warm fuzzies, and because of all the feedback, Emily lives on!

SMOOCH ®

June 2005

Published by

Dorchester Publishing Co., Inc.
200 Madison Avenue
New York, NY 10016

If you purchased this book without a cover you should be aware that this book is stolen property. It was reported as "unsold and destroyed" to the publisher and neither the author nor the publisher has received any payment for this "stripped book."

Copyright © 2005 by Marthe Arends

All rights reserved. No part of this book may be reproduced or transmitted in any form or by any electronic or mechanical means, including photocopying, recording or by any information storage and retrieval system, without the written permission of the publisher, except where permitted by law.

ISBN 0-8439-5549-X

The name "SMOOCH" and its logo are trademarks of Dorchester Publishing Co., Inc.

Printed in the United States of America.

Visit us on the web at www.smoochya.com.

PRAISE FOR KATIE MAXWELL!

"Katie Maxwell has her finger on the pulse of teen girls and is well-versed in what's hot and what's not."
—Roundtable Reviews

GOT FANGS?

"Whether you're a teen, an adult, into paranormal stories or romance books, *Got Fangs?* is a great read for all!"
—*Romance Reviews Today*

"Fran is a hilarious character whose hectic life, and demented mother and friends, will drag readers into this novel, and not let them out until the very last page. Whether you're a fan of Katie Maxwell's or not, *Got Fangs?* is a book that can't be missed!"

—Erika Sorocco, Teen Correspondent

THE TAMING OF THE DRU

"*The Taming of the Dru* is definitely uber-fabu and should be placed on summer reading lists everywhere."
—*RT BOOKclub*

"Emily has won a place in the hearts of anyone who loves to laugh. Her world is weird, wonderful, and very real."
—*Huntress Reviews*

WHAT'S FRENCH FOR "EW!"?

"Katie Maxwell deftly and hilariously delivers a potent message about the most important decisions. Emily is a breath of fresh air, wholly realistic, and utterly charming. If you love the Princess Diaries, this series is equally fun, no matter if you are a teen or once were one."
—*Huntress Reviews*

MORE PRAISE FOR KATIE MAXWELL!

THEY WEAR WHAT ***UNDER THEIR KILTS?***
"Welcome back to the sidesplitting universe of Emily Williams…. [This is] a larky addition that won't disappoint teens hooked by the first book."
—*Booklist*

"A complete blast to read."
—*RT BOOKclub*

"A must-have book, as Emily's antics cannot be missed."
—Erika Sorocco, Teen Correspondent

"Maxwell delivers a character that speaks her mind while making you laugh out loud…. Maxwell's novel is a real trip."
—*The Barnes & Noble Review*

THE YEAR MY LIFE WENT DOWN THE LOO
"*The Year My Life Went Down the Loo* is a treat! Laugh-out-loud funny, full of sly wit and humor, poignant, realistic teenage angst, and expertly drawn characters, the book is impossible to put down."
—*Romance Reviews Today*

"Gripping, smart-alecky, shocking…and at the same time tender. A brilliant debut by Katie Maxwell!"
—*KLIATT*

"Refreshing. It's so true to life, dealing with an average teenage girl's issues instead of the mild and bland subjects covered in many other YA novels. Girls will laugh, sigh and squeal aloud as they embark upon Emily's journey."
—*RT BOOKclub*

Subject: Quiz results—The Art of Being Emily
From: Emster@seattlegrrl.com
To: Hollyberry@britsahoy.co.uk

Instructions: Fill out the quiz below and pass it along to all your friends so they can see the real you!

What is your worst fear? Other than really grotty big hairy spiders, that I don't survive high school graduation. Or snakes. Snakes are bad. Oh, wait, change that—worst fear is that I won't go to college in Canada with Fang. Or that my father will say something so embarrassing in front of my friends that my head explodes. Either of those works.

Are you evil? If I was evil, I'd like snakes and spiders *and* my father.

Have you ever shaved your head? Um. This is a really odd quiz.

Would you rather be an elephant or a tiger? This is a trick question, isn't it? I think we had this in a biology class. I'm pretty sure the answer is 42.

Would you rather freeze to death or be burned alive? Er…this is really, really the most bizarre question ever asked.

How do you feel about your parents? See freeze to death or be burned alive question.

Ever told someone you love him? Fang! Numalicious! Major squeezage! Love, love, love! Must IM him right this second. Rest of the quiz later…

Other SMOOCH books by Katie Maxwell:

The Emily Series:
THE TAMING OF THE DRU
WHAT'S FRENCH FOR "EW!"?
THEY WEAR *WHAT* UNDER THEIR KILTS?
THE YEAR MY LIFE WENT DOWN THE LOO

GOT FANGS?
EYELINER OF THE GODS

Life, Love, and the Pursuit of Hotties

Subject: It's illegal to hire a hit man, right?
From: Emster@seattlegrrl.com
To: Hollyberry@britsahoy.co.uk
Date: June 11, 2005 12:34 pm

I may have to kill Dru.

Hugsies,
~Em

Subject: Re: It's illegal to hire a hit man, right?
From: Emster@seattlegrrl.com
To: Hollyberry@britsahoy.co.uk
Date: June 11, 2005 12:47 pm

> *OMICROD! What's happened now? Why do you*
> *want to kill Dru? Are you done with your classes yet?*
> *Are you excited about graduation? I so wish I was*
> *graduating, too. School just isn't the same without*

> *you. No one ever gets into trouble, or sets off the*
> *sprinklers in the gym, or has a teacher threaten to*
> *have them deported.*

Hey, that thing with Horseface Naylor was blown to-tally out of proportion. She didn't actually threaten to have me deported; she just said she *wished* someone would deport me. There's a big difference.

I've got one more test, then classes are over, woo-hoo! And grad weekend is so going to rock—I can't wait to see Fang. I think some of the senior class thought it was a bit weird that we're going to Vancou-ver rather than that bed-and-breakfast in the San Juan Islands that Miss Pushy "I Have a Pilgrim Name and was Senior Prom Queen and You weren't Nyah Nyah Nyah" Patience wanted, but boo-hoo, I won, she lost, and we're going to Vancouver in a week!

But I may still have to kill Dru.

Huggables,
~Em

Subject: Re: Yes, it is illegal to hire a hit man
From: Emster@seattlegrrl.com
To: Hollyberry@britsahoy.co.uk
Date: June 11, 2005 12:58 pm

> *WHY DO YOU HAVE TO KILL DRU?*

Oooh, shouting in e-mail! That's so ballsy of you. Hee! Ballsy! OK, acting adult here. Dru has gone off the deep end with this wedding thing. I thought at first all the wedding planning was kind of fun—I mean, how cool is it to go to a bridal store and try on wedding dresses (and in my case, maid of honor dresses)? But then Felix left to do his four year military thing, and Dru just isn't coping well. Rather than admitting that she won't be getting married until after he gets back, she's in some sort of bridal denial!

"Dru, I'm your oldest and best friend," I told her two days ago as we were doing commencement practice (shaking hands with one hand and accepting a diploma with the other). "You know I have only your best interests at heart."

"Yeah," she said, shoving a piece of paper at me. "No, Em, shake with your right; take the diploma with your left. It's not that hard."

"You're not using your left hand to diploma me!"

"Yes, I am. See?" She turned around so she was facing in the same direction as me.

I narrowed my eyes at her hand with the fake diploma. "Oh. It didn't look right."

"That's because it's not; it's left," she said, shaking the piece of paper.

"I know that. I meant it didn't look right that your left was right."

She blinked at me a couple of times. "Huh?"

3

"The right hand. It didn't look right to me that your left hand was the right hand."

Her mouth dropped open a little bit. "Em, are you, like, on drugs? 'Cause that just didn't make any sense!"

"Oh, ha, ha, very funny, Miss Comedian." I snatched the fake diploma and stuffed it underneath my mattress.

"Well, what did you mean then?"

I opened my mouth to tell her, but I couldn't think of a way to explain that didn't involve a whiteboard and five colored pens. "Never mind."

"Sheesh, Em. How do you expect to become a world renowned astrophysicist before you're twenty-five if you can't even tell your left from your right?"

"So I got a little mixed up! So what? I have things on my mind! Important things, like why Fang doesn't love me anymore!"

She rolled her eyes and dug the pretend diploma out from the bed. "Oh, man, we're not going to go back to 'Fang Doesn't Love Me Land' again, are we? Because I'm going to need white cheddar popcorn and a six pack of diet Coke if we are."

"He hasn't called me in three weeks! *Three whole weeks!*"

"Oh, that's nothing. Felix hasn't called me in a month, and you don't see me having a meltdown."

"That's because he's at boot camp and not allowed to call you! But this is different! Omigod! Look how upset I am! I'm speaking in exclamation points!"

She laughed and whapped me on the arm with the

paper. "You're such an idiot at times, Em. Fang e-mails you every day, and that's more than I get from Felix. Now do it again. Right hand shake, left hand take. It's easy as pie."

I wanted to make mean eyes at her, but I couldn't, because even I knew it was stupid to try to pretend that Fang didn't love me. I sighed a tragic *Camille*-like sigh instead, and did the shake-and-take thing.

She didn't let go of the diploma. "Em."

"What?" I asked, wondering if someone would write an opera about my sad life—only without the tuberculosis and the dying part. I bet if I were dying Fang would call me.

"What are you doing?"

I looked. The diploma was in my right hand. "Gah! I'm dyslexic or something! Stress has done this to me! I can't take it anymore! Oh, no, I'm talking in exclamation points again! Double gah with antlers on!"

Dru looked at me with her head tipped to one side. "You know, you do look a bit stressed out lately."

"I am! Totally stressed!"

"I know just what you need to relax," she said, grabbing her purse and turning it upside down on my bed.

Now, you've met Dru, so you know how she is about purses—she doesn't like to go anywhere without taking enough stuff to cover any emergency, from Mr. Monthly Visitor suddenly appearing, to possible death by starvation on a mountain in Chile, like those soccer guys that Brother is always going on about whenever Mom tries to make him eat brussels sprouts, telling him he's going to get some sort of horrible old-guy disease if he doesn't eat more leafy green stuff, at which point Brother says he'd rather die a cannibal than eat miniature wads of gack (i.e., the brussels sprouts). Which I totally understand, because you know I hate them, too, although I do like asparagus, and Brother claims they are alien pod-spears dropped on earth to turn everyone into alien pod spear people. Honestly, I think Brother is going senile. It's not his whole deal with insisting everyone call him Brother instead of his real name—I can understand the importance of having a cool name! Mom says he's just eccentric and it's part of his charm, but I'm thinking it's time to start looking into some professional old-person care for him, which is just sad, because I don't know anyone else's father who is deranged.

Where was I? Oh, yeah, Dru's purse. She had to shake it to get everything out, because there was so much wadded in there, it was like a dense black hole of Dru stuff.

"What, I need you to dump stuff all over my bed so I can appreciate the fact that I don't tote around approximately one hundred and seventy-two pounds of . . . Hey! Isn't that my bottle of smelly perfume that I don't like, but have to keep because Fang gave it to me for Christmas?"

Dru shoved aside a pair of sparkly pink ankle socks (no comment . . . although you know how bad she looks in pink!), three lipsticks, her hairbrush and matching comb, a big mirror, her *Brides Now!* journal, and a bottle of water, pulling out the purple bottle of perfume that Fang had given me. "Oh, yeah, I was returning it, and forgot. Thanks for letting me borrow it. You're right—it does make you smell like you're your own grandma."

I put the perfume on my dresser, right next to Fang's picture, blowing him a little smooch because he was so thoughtful to try to get me something he thought I'd like (this year I'm giving him an annotated list of my wants, complete with URLs to Web sites where he can buy the stuff).

"Oh, here it is," Dru said, pulling out an object from the wad o' stuff.

I narrowed my eyes at it. "That looks suspiciously like a magazine."

She scooped everything else back into her purse, dropping it on the floor as she plopped onto the bed, patting the spot next to her. "This always makes me feel better when I get a bit stressy. Come and sit."

"That's not what I think it is, is it?" I asked, moving cautiously toward my desk where my birthday present from Bess was kept (I can't tell you how handy it is to have a sister who is Wiccan).

Dru smoothed the magazine cover and smiled at it. "We haven't done this in a long time, Em."

I reached for the drawer, careful not to turn my back on her (never turn your back on someone armed with the horrible tool of destruction that Dru had). My hand felt around the drawer for the protection charm Bess had made me. "Dru, tell me it's not what I think it is. Tell me it's not that most horrible of all things . . . tell me it's not—"

She smiled a big old piranha smile and held the magazine up so I could see the cover. "*Young Bride* magazine! Let's pick out our dream wedding outfits!"

"Gah!" I yelled, spinning around to jerk the drawer out. It was empty. "Oh, no, not again! Dermott! Stop hiding my stuff and give me back that charm! It's the only thing that can save me from the horror of bride magazines!"

Dru cackled (honest to God, she cackled! That's what bride magazines do to you! Stay away from them at all costs!), and said, "You don't really believe your underwear drawer ghost followed you home all the way from England?"

I opened all the other drawers to find the charm. They were all empty too. Lately Dermott has taken to hiding things from me—it's his newest game. Normally I don't mind, unless it's something important, like my Victoria's Secret stuff, but this was going too far! I needed that protection charm to save me from the evil influence of bride stuff!

"Thus speaketh someone who doesn't have a ghost haunting her undies," I said with much dignity, looking around my room, trying to figure out where Dermott would put the things from the desk. I checked my dresser, but that just had clothes and the usual stuff. I sighed. "Ideas, Dru?"

"Hmm?" She looked up from the magazine, a glazed look in her eyes (I'm telling you—those things are pure evil!).

"Ideas on where Dermott has hidden the stuff from my desk?"

"Oh." She looked around the room. "Shoes."

"Huh?"

"If I were a ghost, I'd hide things in shoes. But you know, Em, I think you're way off with this ghost being Dermott. We released him! We did the séances and everything, and you had a whole ton of frogs in your room for days in order to release his spirit to a higher plane and all that biz. If you are haunted—and I'm kinda skeptical about that, Em, because I haven't seen any signs of a ghost—then it's got to be a different one."

"Shoes," I said scornfully, but not having any better idea, I went to look in the closet.

"Yup. That's where I'd put stuff," she said, going back to her mag. "Oooh, centerpieces made out of ice! I could have portraits of Felix and me done in ice! That would be so fabu!"

I pulled a small heart-shaped muslin bag from my pointy-toed ankle boot. "Wow. You were right, Dru. Good call!"

"You know I'm majorly psychic," she said, turning the page. "Oooooooooh! Hand-painted cakes! Em, you have to see this! Oh, and there are the sweetest brides-maids dresses I found—they would be so cool! Let me show you. You're going to love them—you could wear them after the wedding for parties and stuff."

I sat down next to her on the bed, clutching my protection charm. "Dru, honey, sweetie . . . we need to have a little talk. It's tough-love time, babe."

"I know I sticky-noted the page with the bridesmaid dresses," she muttered to herself, flipping through the magazine. One side of it bristled with sticky-note tabs. "Maybe this is . . . no, that's the push-up bra I want."

"I know you're upset about Felix going ahead with his plan to join the army so he'll have college paid for when he gets out. I understand that. If I were engaged and my fiancé did that, I'd have the hissy fit to end all hissy fits. But you didn't hissy at all—and that worries me, Dru, because if anyone deserves the title of Class Drama Queen, it's you."

She glared at me over the top of the magazine. "I am *so* not the one in this room who is the drama queen, Miss Talking in Exclamation Points."

I lifted my chin and tried to look down my nose at her, like Brother does when those religious guys come around to the door trying to get him to join their church. "Hello! There is a big difference between stressing because your BF hasn't called you in three weeks—that's three whole, entire weeks. Consecutive weeks!—and pretending that stuff that has happened hasn't really happened."

"I don't know what you're talking about," she said, immersing herself in the mag again. "I'm engaged. I'm getting married."

"Yeah, but not for four years! I know you want to plan your wedding, and yeah, I admit it was fun at first to think about it, but you're obsessing about it now!"

"Look," she said, turning the magazine around so I could see a page she'd marked. "I know you liked the slinky red dresses for bridesmaids, but I've rethought the red-and-black color scheme and I think this is much, much better."

I stared in horror at the page. "You can't be serious."

"Of course I am," she said, smiling at the page. "They're soft, very feminine colors, don't you think? They'll look good on everyone."

My skin crawled, Holly. I swear, it *crawled*. "Individually, yeah. The pale yellow is nice. The mauve would be nice with the right accessories. And I suppose if I had to, if world peace or something like that were on the line, the mint green is survivable. I mean, I'd have to ritually burn the dress after the wedding, but I would wear it. But no, Dru, no, no, no. No to the eighteenth power—a bridesmaid dress in yellow, mauve, and mint-green plaid is just wrong!"

"I think they're pretty," she said, smoothing down the page.

"It violates the laws of nature," I told her, squeezing the charm to get a bit of extra protection from it in case the evil bride magazine tried to take my brain like it took Dru's.

"They're spring colors, and you're a spring."

"That dress makes my eyeballs want to bleed," I said.

"It probably violates international human rights treaties. I bet just looking at it is classified as cruel and unusual punishment."

"It's *my* wedding."

"If you live to see it, and I'm telling you right here and now, I am not going to be responsible for keeping the other bridesmaids from killing you if you try to foist that dress on us."

"Omicrod." She gasped, her eyes huge (glazed huge, not normal huge). "I could get matching tablecloths and napkins!"

I left the room after that. There was no other choice—even Bess's most powerful protection charm couldn't save me from a force as strong as Dru in wedding-planning mode.

Sigh again. You see what I mean? If Dru is serious about those bridesmaid dresses, death will be the only option. It will be merciful. No jury in the world would convict me, right?

Whoops, gotta run. Time for a quick trip to the mall to buy a few things for grad weekend.

Huggles and all,
~Em

Subject: Re: Surprise!
From: Emster@seattlegrrl.com
To: Devonator@skynetcomm.com
Date: June 11, 2005 6:12 pm

> *thought I would surprise you by just showing up, but*
> *Fang said it would be better to let your parents know*
> *ahead of time. So can you ask them for me? If there's*
> *no room or something, that's cool. I can stay at a ho-*
> *tel. It'll be just for a week; then I'm going to see Fang*
> *for a few days, then on to Ontario to see a cousin of*
> *my mom's for ten days.*

Omicrod! Oh, my crod!!!!! With five exclamation points, because I'm just that excited! You're coming to Seattle! Woo-hooooooooo! I've got goose bumps! I actually have goose bumps, because the only thing better than seeing you would be seeing Fang. Wait. That sounded rude, didn't it? I didn't mean it that way! It's just that he's my BF, and although you're my former BF and all, Fang rates a little higher on the squee meter.

Regardless of that, *squeeeee!* You're coming to Seattle! Oh! Wait! You said you're leaving on Wednesday? Oh, no! Oh, no, oh, no, oh, no! I'm going to be gone Friday through Sunday on my grad weekend. I told you about that, right? How hard I had to work to get everyone to finally agree to go to Vancouver (that's in British Columbia—right next to the town where Fang's college is) rather than some snotty bed-and-breakfast in the San

Juans (they're local islands—pretty, but boring after you've looked at a couple of whales and stuff). Gah! That means I'll miss three whole days of your week in Seattle!

Excited anyway hugs,
~Em

Subject: Guess what?
From: Emster@seattlegrrl.com
To: Hwilliams@ewedub.edu
Date: June 11, 2005 6:13 pm

Hey, Brother, guess who's coming to Seattle and needs a place to stay for a week? It's Devon! Isn't that great? I'm so excited! He'll be coming on Wednesday. You don't mind picking him up at the airport, do you? I've got my last paper on the Cold War due on Thursday, and I really, really, really need every spare minute to do it, because the Cold War is soooo yesterday I can hardly keep my eyes open.

I'll tell Mom that he's coming so she can get all the naked-people pictures out of the spare bedroom. When is she going to get over this porno painting kick, do you know? I almost died the last time I went in there and she was looking at a video of naked guys standing around posing. I mean, that's just not *normal!*

Hugums,
~Em

Subject: re: Guess what?
From: Emster@seattlegrrl.com
To: Hwilliams@ewedub.edu
Date: June 11, 2005 6:15 pm

> *Sure, why not, it's not like I have anything important*
> *of my own to do, like writing the definitive analysis of*
> *family life during the high Middle Ages. I did mention*
> *that book at dinner some months ago, did I not? The*
> *one I am contracted to write by a very renowned and*
> *respected academic publisher? The one due in Sep-*
> *tember?*

Fine, I'll pick him up myself, but you remember that when I receive a 3.7 instead of the 3.95 I should be getting in U.S. history.

> *Not to mention which, the Eisenhower years and the*
> *cold war were defining events in twentieth century*
> *history, one which has lessons to be learned that are*
> *still relevant in*

[Snipped 'cause I only have so much brain I can devote to history, and it's crammed full of stupid 1950s stuff right now.]
So you're serious about not picking up Devon?

> *as for your mother's paintings, they are not porno-*
> *graphic, although I admit that the one with the two*

> *women wrestling was a bit . . . Never mind. Nudes*
> *have long been a respected element in the fine arts,*
> *Emily. For someone who claims to have an open*
> *mind, I'm surprised you object so strenuously to*
> *your mother indulging in her interest in painting*
> *them.*

I have the openest mind of everyone I know, but cheese on rye, Brother! Do you have any idea how embarrassing it is to have your best friend see that your mom spends all her time painting nakies? Everyone thinks she has a complex or something! Gah!

Doomed to a horrible grade in history because of a heartless father,
~Em

Subject: re: Guess what?
From: Emster@seattlegrrl.com
To: Hwilliams@ewedub.edu
Date: June 11, 2005 6:16 pm

> *Emily, you are aware of the fact that I am currently*
> *sitting in a room approximately twenty feet from you,*
> *yes? Has our relationship degraded to the point*
> *where you have to e-mail me rather than expend the*
> *effort to cross the room to the door, open it, and*
> *speak to me directly?*

Yes. You refuse to use an instant messenger, so e-mail is it. You seriously need to get with the times, Brother. Just because you specialize in medieval history doesn't mean you have to be medieval, too. You're the only father I know who doesn't IM. Even Dru's dad, who is so computer illiterate he thought the CD tray on the computer was a cup holder, uses an IM.

She with the backward father,
~Em

Subject: re: Sorry, love
From: Emster@seattlegrrl.com
To: Fbaxter@doormouse.ca
Date: June 11, 2005 10:22 pm

> *Sorry I didn't have a chance to e-mail you before this.*
> *Dr. Wu had me go with her on a call to a local pig*
> *farm, and by the time we got back, I was all in.*
> *What's up with you? How is your paper going? You*
> *only have a couple more days left, right?*

Smoochie face!
Ugh. OK. That just sounded stupid.
Fangycakes!
Hmm. That's not much better, is it? *Le* sigh. OK, how about just: Fang!
You're excused for not e-mailing me first thing this

morning like you usually do, although why were you all in from going to a pig farm? I mean, ick on the whole pig farm thing (you didn't have to see them being killed and stuff, did you? Because if you did, I'd understand not wanting to do anything but forget what I saw), but that's not like you to be all-in-ish just for going out with your vet teacher. What did you have to do there? Wait—if it has anything to do with chopping things off, I don't want to know. But if it was something fun, like looking at baby pigs, then you can tell me. Just remember that I'm still a bit twitchy from that museum job last summer where I was surrounded by dead things.

Blech.

My paper is going. I can't wait to be done with school. More than normal—here I am, poised on the threshold of bigger and better things (a.k.a. college), and I'm stuck for one last week in high school hell. Oh, well, there's the grad weekend to look forward to, and then—are you keeping track?—only three weeks to our cruise! It'll be a double helping of Fang for me, yay!

Kissies galore,
Emily (who goes all melty over the whole "love" thing)

You have a Chat Girl Instant Message. Click to receive it.

GonnaMarryFelix: Hey, Em, did you hear from Fang?

Em=c^2: Yup, just did. He said he's all in from visiting some pigs. What do you think that means?

GonnaMarryFelix: I think that means he's tired. Isn't that an English phrase?

Em=c^2: /me gives Dru a pointed look.

Em=c^2: Well, of course it means he's tired. But how could seeing pigs make you tired? I think something's wrong.

GonnaMarryFelix: You're just like my mom, worrying about stuff that hasn't happened. What could be wrong with Fang?

Em=c^2: I don't know; that's why I'm asking you. Maybe he's homesick? What if he wants . . . eeeeeeeeeeeek! What if he misses Audrey!

GonnaMarryFelix: /me rolls eyes.

GonnaMarryFelix: You said their breakup was really final, and Fang didn't mind that Audrey went home to New Zealand.

Em=c^2: Yeah, but things can change!

GonnaMarryFelix: I am not going to play the "he loves me, he doesn't love me" game with you anymore! The last time you sucked me into that, I ended up calling Fang and asking him if he still loved you, and he laughed at me. At me! That was the most embarrassing thing you've ever made me do. Stop being so paranoid. If he says he's tired, he's just tired. It doesn't mean he is in love with someone else.

Em=c^2: /me sighs.

Em=c^2: You're right.

GonnaMarryFelix: What?!?!

Em=c^2: I said you're right, OK? Criminy, don't make a federal case out of it.

GonnaMarryFelix: Wow. Gotta take a screen shot of this. Emily admitting someone else is right . . .

Em=c^2: So funny I forgot to laugh. All right, all right, I'll stop worrying about Fang. I'm sure you're right—he probably stayed up late or something the night before.

Em=c^2: . . .

GonnaMarryFelix: Hmm?

Em=c^2: I'm thinking. " . . . " means I'm thinking.

GonnaMarryFelix: Oh.

Em=c^2: . . .

Em=c^2: What is he doing staying up late, do you think? He said this quarter was really intense, with all sorts of practical work and interning with his assigned vet—why would he be up late if he has to do animal stuff?

GonnaMarryFelix: He's a guy. Guys party. Felix hardly ever goes to bed before three in the morning. Are you done with your paper on the Cold War?

Em=c^2: No. Party? You really think he's out partying? With other, you know, women and stuff?

GonnaMarryFelix: Oh, no, now you're going jealous. You know, Em, you used to be so cool about Fang and everything, and now you've gone typical GF. It's like you're regressing or something.

Em=c^2: Waaaaaaaaaah! I can't help it! Everything has been so good for six months, ever since Fang moved to BC just so we could be nearer each other. He's the best boyfriend anyone could ever have—he's sweet, and adorable, and he has those puppy-dog eyes that melt me, and *omicrod,* his lips ought to be registered with the FBI, because if I were a spy and he kissed me, I'd tell him everything I knew, and probably a lot of stuff I didn't know.

GonnaMarryFelix: If everything is so perfect in Emily-and-Fang-Land, why are you worrying?

Em=c^2: /me gives Dru another look.

GonnaMarryFelix: What?

Em=c^2: Sheesh, Dru, I've talked to you about this for the last month! I told you all about how worried I was because everything was so perfect, that I was sure something horrible was coming, because that's how things always work in my life. Weren't you paying attention at all?

GonnaMarryFelix: I've been busy planning the wedding. . . .

Em=c^2: No wedding talk! No! Wedding! Talk! My brain will explode if you do any more wedding talk!

GonnaMarryFelix: You're so strange, Emily. I swear, you changed when you were in England. You used to be fun. Now you're . . .

Em=c^2: Mature?

GonnaMarryFelix: . . . eccentric.

Em=c^2: Oh! You don't have to get insulting!

GonnaMarryFelix: I didn't mean it to be an insult. It's just that . . .

Em=c^2: What?

GonnaMarryFelix: Well . . . you're getting like your father. Kind of . . . odd.

Em=c^2: Aaaaaaaaaack! I'm not talking to you anymore, not until you take that back! I am not turning into Brother!

GonnaMarryFelix: I'm not going to take back something that's the truth!

Em=c^2: Dru!!!!!

GonnaMarryFelix: OK, maybe you're not turning into him, but you're sure heading that way.

Em=c^2: I am not! Brother is downright weird. He has strange hobbies.

GonnaMarryFelix: Like sword fighting—how's the scar where you got into a duel with Fang's ex?

Em=c^2: And he talks strange deliberately.

GonnaMarryFelix: Are you still saying "shedyule" for schedule, and calling the bathroom the loo?

Em=c^2: And he has bizarre friends who I swear aren't really human.

GonnaMarryFelix: Six words: Dermott the eighteenth-century English ghost.

Em=c^2: Gaaaah!

GonnaMarryFelix: You'd better watch it, Em. Any day now you're going to decide to switch from physics to medieval history, and then all will be lost.

Em=c^2: Gaaaaaaaaaah!
GonnaMarryFelix: I'm going to go work on my paper.
Em=c^2: Fine. I'll just sit here and be *weird*.
GonnaMarryFelix: Later, Em.
Em=c^2: Wah!

Subject: Um . . . is there something I should know?
From: Emster@seattlegrrl.com
To: Fbaxter@doormouse.ca
Date: June 12, 2005 6:57 am

Fang, you know if there's anything you need to tell me, I'll understand, right? If something is going on with you that you want to tell, you can. 'Cause you know that I won't freak out or anything if you have something . . . uh . . . bad to tell me. I mean, I won't be happy to hear it, but if you need to tell me, you should. Tell me, that is. So don't be afraid to let me know if anything . . . bad . . . is going on with you.

Crap, I have to go now or I'll be late for school. Major smoochies, and lots and lots of I-can-take-it hugs,

Emily

Subject: re: Um . . . is there something I should know?
From: Emster@seattlegrrl.com
To: Fbaxter@doormouse.ca
Date: June 11, 2005 3:19 pm

> *That was one of your more bizarre e-mails. I had to*
> *read it three times before I figured out that you think*
> *I'm seeing someone else—is that it? If it is, you can*
> *just stop thinking that, because there's no one else*
> *for me but you.*

Oh, man, how can regular words like that make me go so melty inside? You know that there's no other guy for me, either. You make my stomach turn somersaults whenever I see your picture, and after you call me I sing a lot for days and days. In fact, the last time you called (three weeks ago, in case you were wondering), Brother went off on yet another one of his hissy fits.

"What are you singing about now?" Brother asked as I did a little impromptu song and dance down the stairs (sounds weird, but I was just so happy hearing your voice, I had to do a dance routine or I would have exploded or burst into spontaneous combustion, or something like that). He was standing at the bottom of the stairs, going through the mail, his hair horn extra horny, because he's letting his hair grow. Mom says he's going through a midlife crisis. I say he's just nuts, because old guys should not have long hair. It would look good on you (in case you wanted to grow yours out), but on Brother? Bleh.

"Fang called," I sang, doing a little dance around him because I was so happy, not even his jumbo hair horn could depress me. "Fang called, Fang called, Faaaaaaaaang caaaaaaaalled . . ."

"Lord preserve me from young girls in love," Brother said, trying to get around me, but I grabbed his hands.

"Dance with me, Brother," I said, doing a couple of really cool dance steps like what's-her-face in *Havana Nights*.

"Em—"

"Come on, don't be so old and stodgy you can't dance when Fang calls," I said, doing a twirl around him.

"I've written a whole chapter pertinent to you, you know," Brother said, narrowing his eyes as I dragged him after me in an attempt to make him dance. "Ostensibly it's about how fathers in the Middle Ages dealt with irksome daughters, sending them to convents or marrying them off before they were thirteen, but in reality it's all about how daughters can make their fathers' lives sheer and utter hell, a subject I'm all too conversant with."

"I bet you those fathers didn't dance when their daughters boyfriends called, either," I sang, letting go of him for a minute to give in to happy feet. "I bet you those fathers died early deaths due to stress-caused heart attacks."

"They didn't have stress in the Middle Ages," Brother said (grumpily).

"Ha! They had plagues"—I jumped on the seat of the hall stand and flung myself off in a really cool move—"and boils"—I broke into a tap dance, and tapped a circle around Brother—"and oozing pustules. If that doesn't cause stress, I don't know what does."

Brother sighed, tossed the mail, and grabbed my hands as I stopped tapping and started Time Warping. "Fine, we'll dance, but we'll do a proper dance."

"Eeek," I screamed, freezing up. "Not an old people's dance! No waltzing or something like that."

"Don't be ridiculous—I don't know how to waltz. If you want to dance, we'll do the saltarello."

Now, you're probably Googling the saltarello, so I'll save you the trouble and tell you that it's a really old dance that Brother made Bess and me learn years ago when we were little. It's actually kind of fun, because you get to do a lot of jumping around, and you can do freestyle leaps and high kicks and stuff. Bess used to go wild with it when she was doing ballet. Brother says it's a court dance, but it's nothing like those boring dances that they did at first in *A Knight's Tale* (you know, before they started the cool dancing). So Brother and I saltarelloed around the downstairs hall, and I added a little hip action, because there is only so much old stuff a girl can take without going insane.

"See? A little dancing is good for you," I said a few minutes later as Brother collapsed onto the seat of the hall stand, panting and clutching one hand to his chest. I did a couple more twirls. "And it's all because Fang caaaaaaaaaaaalled. I can't wait until I get to go to college. I can't wait until I move to the same town he's living in. I can't wait until I can see him every day, and every night, and we can—"

Whoops! Almost went a bit too far there.

"God help me," Brother said, his shoulders slumping as he dropped his head into his hands. "Eighteen years old, and she's already planning on cohabitating with her boy toy."

"He's not a boy toy. He's a man toy," I pointed out, doing one last round of happy feet. "He's almost twenty-three."

Brother lifted his head and glared at me. "Is that supposed to make me feel better?"

I stopped dancing and put my hands on my hips. "You're not going to have the sex talk with me again, are you? Honestly, Brother, sometimes I think you're sex obsessed!"

"Me?" He gasped, running one hand through his hair horn. "I'm not the one doing a libertine dance around the hall while planning on engaging in sexual congress with a boy old enough to be her . . . her . . ."

"Boyfriend?" I sang, giving in and twirling one last time. "Brother, I've already told you and Mom at least five million times this summer that Fang and I aren't going to do anything like that. Yet."

"Good," Brother said, giving me a suspicious glance. "Wait—yet? What's that supposed to mean?"

I grinned. "I'm eighteen now. I'll be going to college

in three months. I'll be living on my own, with no parents to answer to, and my sweet, adorable, love bunny of a BF just a few minutes away from me. Who knows what will happen then?"

"Chris!" Brother yelled, looking around me to the door that led to the kitchen. "Has the check for Emily's tuition cleared yet? If not, call the bank and put a hold on it. She can go to a junior college here until she's thirty."

"Ha, ha," I laughed, wapping Brother on the arm. "Ha, ha, ha, ha, ha. Not. Besides, Mom won't let me register yet."

"Emily," he said, getting that serious father look on his face that he gets whenever he wants to talk about creepy stuff like sex (not that sex is creepy, but talking to your father about it is). "I know you think you're mature beyond your years, but there is much more to life than just bonging your boyfriend."

"It's boinking, Brother, and I'm not going to do the sex talk with you now because I'm too happy, and I don't want to have to go get the big bag o' condoms that you and Mom and Bess have given me over the last year or so just to prove to you that yes, I know all about safe sex and STDs and HIV and other stuff. So let's just move on and I'll go dance my way to the library, and you do old-guy stuff until Mom can slip you valium or something."

"Chris," Brother yelled again as I shuffle-kick-spinned my way up the stairs. "Emily has promised me that you will feed me valium. Do you have enough to put me to sleep for the next ten years? I suspect I'm going to be better off sedated than living through Emily's antics. . . ."

I stopped listening to him at that point, because you know how Brother is—he never, ever stops talking. He can go on and on and on about the most boring stuff, things no other person in the whole world would even spend a nanosecond talking about, but which Brother yammers on about forever. I think it's hereditary, because my grandma talks just as much as he does. And, well, we both know how Bess is.

Where was I? Oh, yeah, I was telling you how happy I am when I hear your voice. Should I call you tonight? I've got almost fifteen minutes left on my free long distance, so if you're not going to be studying or dissecting animals or all that other stuff you do, I can call you.

Kisses, kisses, kisses!
Emily

Subject: Re: You're going on a cruise? A real cruise???
From: Emster@seattlegrrl.com
To: Hollyberry@britsahoy.co.uk
Date: June 14, 2005 11:12 pm

> *didn't tell me about a cruise! A cruise on one of those*
> *big ships, you mean? La vache!*

Hee. I still giggle when I say *la vache!* Studying in Paris last year was too cool! Hey, have you heard anything from the Gruesome Twins we endured there? I got an e-mail from Sabine saying she and her weirdo twin were going to Bryn Mawr (that's an all-girls—excuse me, -women—college on the East Coast—overrated, IMHO, but lots of people seem to like it), and was I going to Harvard like I planned.

E-mail from me: "I've changed my plans—I'm going to a college in British Columbia so I can be nearer to my boyfriend. And it's costing a lot less because college in Canada is less expensive."

E-mail from her: "Too bad you didn't get into Harvard. Good luck with the hick college."

Me: grinds teeth.

Anyway, back to the cruise! I can't believe I didn't tell you about it! I mean, it's just the biggest thing that's happened to me all year! Why wouldn't I tell you . . . ? Oh, wait! I know why I didn't tell you. I won the cruise in April, when you were in Italy with your parents. I must have forgotten to tell you when you got back because I wasn't absotively sure I was going to get to use the cruise.

Question: Why is my life so difficult?

Answer: My father makes it that way.

Back in January the fam and I went to this big crafts fair. I didn't want to go, but Mom had entered some ceramic stuff in it, and Brother dragged Bess and me along so we could make a big deal about Mom getting an award in Best Depiction of Nude People on a Liver-wurst Tray, or something like that (honestly, you just don't want to know). Anyhoo, there were all sorts of vendors and stuff to buy things from, and one of them was for a place that was giving away a cruise.

Now, I'm not an idiot. I know that sometimes those contests have hidden stuff that you have to be careful of. So I asked the guy who was running it (kinda nerdy—prolly a 5.6 on the hottie scale) what the deal was.

"This is just a contest to win a cruise, right?" I asked, squinting at the tiny print on the back of the entry form. "I don't have to buy anything?"

"You are not obligated to purchase anything at any time," the guy said, flashing me a toothy smile. "If you win, we simply ask you to attend a short presentation, and then you can collect your prize."

"What sort of presentation?" I asked, suspicious.

"Do you like to travel?" the guy asked.

"Yeah. We just got back from a year in England, as a matter of fact. And I spent some time studying French in Paris." That always sounds so cool. People here get impressed when you tell them you studied in Paris.

"Then you'll love our presentation featuring luxury accommodations around the world," the guy assured me. I double checked the back of the form, but it said right on it in big letters—NO PURCHASE NECESSARY TO WIN!

So a couple of months go by, and one night I get a phone call.

"This is Em. Speak!" I commanded when I answered my cell phone (I was in one of those moods).

"Hello, I'm calling for Ms. Williams. Ms. Emily Williams?"

"You got her."

"Congratulations, Ms. Williams, you are a winner!"

"Coolio!" I said, thinking . . . well, coolio! I mean, I won something! You know I never, ever win anything! "Umm . . . what contest did I win?"

"Do you remember entering a contest at a craft fair? Well, your name was picked from the hundreds of entrants, and you have won one of five Extremely Valuable Prizes," the woman said, and just the way she talked you could tell she was capitalizing those words.

"Oooh, fabu," I said, trying to remember what the contest was for.

"It is indeed fabulous. You are a *very* lucky woman to be chosen! These five Extremely Valuable Prizes are highly sought after, and I just know you'll enjoy whichever prize you pick. Now, I need to verify a few things before we move forward with information on how you can collect your EVP." She didn't actually say EVP, but I'm tired of writing it out.

"OK," I said, and confirmed that yes, I was really Emily Williams, and yes, I lived at my current addy, and I was a U.S. citizen, and at least eighteen years of age. "Um . . . yeah."

The woman hesitated. "Is something I listed incorrect?"

I looked at my Jude Law calendar. It was the fifth, and my birthday was less than two weeks away. I would be eighteen then. "Erm . . . when did you say I needed to collect my EVP?"

"I have several dates open between now and the end of the month," the woman said briskly. "But before I can book a date for you, I need to have your verbal verification that the information you gave us is accurate and up-to-date."

I breathed out a silent sigh of relief. If I could get a date to pick up my EVP after the eighteenth of the month, I'd be fine. So I could say yes then, because by the time I went in to get it, it would be all true. "Sure thing. It's all correct." Or it would be in a couple of weeks.

"Excellent! Now, let me reiterate that you are already a winner, and you will have your choice from five EVPs once you get to our corporate headquarters. Let me give you our available dates when you can come to select your prize." She rattled off a number of dates. I picked one right at the end of the month, just because it made me feel better about fibbing about my age now. I mean, I'd be *really* eighteen by then.

"Groovy cool. I'll be there."

"There is just one more question I need to verify. Is your annual income currently over thirty-six thousand dollars per year?"

Eeep!

"Um . . ." I said, mentally adding up all the money from my job at Brother's history department (if you can call scanning pictures a job . . . I call it a waste of time, but hey, they're paying me to do it, so whatever).

"Naturally that means your total family income," she said quickly. "If your own personal income is not quite that much, we are quite willing to consider joint income."

"Oh. Well, yeah, I'm sure that's all right," I said. Brother was a professor—he had to make that much. And Mom was selling her paintings and stuff, although not for very much. Still, it all added up.

"I see on your entry that you are not married."

"No, I'm a student."

"Ah, a college student? Excellent. Would you happen to have a parent or guardian who would come with you on the twenty-ninth to pick up your EVP?"

"Eh . . ."

"It's just for legal purposes," the contest woman said in a really confidential tone. "We don't want anyone accusing us of giving Extremely Valuable Prizes to minors. Ha, ha, ha, ha, ha."

"Ha," I said, chewing on my lip. "Well, I suppose I could ask one of my parents—"

"That would be wonderful. We'll see you at one P.M. on the twenty-ninth, then!"

"Yeah, but why do I need a parent—"

"Until then, count yourself lucky! You are a winner!"

She hung up before I could ask any more questions. I looked down at my "I *heart* Josh Hartnett" notepad, where I'd written down the address and directions she'd given me. It was in Seattle, so it shouldn't take long to go pick up my EVP. I remembered by then that the contest I'd entered had been for a cruise, so Brother or Mom would just have to suck it up and come with me to pick up my cruise prize.

I announced that I was a lucky winner that night at dinner. "Mom, can you come with me to pick up my EVP?" I asked after explaining the whole thing.

"I'm afraid not, Em. I have a retreat with my painting class scheduled for that day. Your father can take you."

"What?" Brother said, looking up from a history magazine he had propped up against his water glass. "What sort of horrible thing have you just volunteered me for on the basis that I spawned that man-crazed girl?"

"Hello, I am so not man-crazed! I have a boyfriend! One single, solitary boyfriend! One BF does not man-crazed make, elderly-type person!"

He narrowed his eyes at me. "Elderly!" he said, his nostrils going into flare mode (never a pretty sight, and potentially deadly when you're trying to eat).

"Man-crazed!" I said, giving him just as outraged a look, but without any undue nasal foliage.

"Break it up, you two," Mom said. "Brother, Emily has won some sort of prize, and she needs you to help her to pick it up. It's on the twenty-ninth."

He gave me a suspicious look, but in the end muttered something about taking me. So a few weeks later we rolled up to the addy the woman had given me.

It was in a business park, and it took us a bit to find the place, but at last I walked into the offices of Vacation Paradiso to claim my EVP.

That's when Brother went nuts. Well, more nuts, since we both know he's not running on all six thrusters.

"Hello! I'm Tony, and I'll be your prize facilitator for the next three hours—"

"*Christus sanctus,*" Brother swore (it's Latin—don't ask), his eyes getting huge as he backed away from the tall, skinny guy walking toward us with his hand out. He wasn't at all my type (not that I'm looking when I have the nummiest BF alive), but what gave me the willies was the happy, happy, I'm-on-some-serious-mood-altering-drugs smile that was plastered all over Tony's face. "This is a . . . a . . . *timeshare!*"

"Huh?" I asked, trying to look like I wasn't with Brother. I thought he was going to whip out a cross and hold it up all Dracula-like. I pinched his arm and hissed through my teeth so no one would hear, "Brother, you're embarrassing me. It's just a cheesy smile, for Pete's sake. You don't have to make such a big deal about it."

"Timeshare," Brother wailed, grabbing me and trying to push me toward the door.

"Why, yes, we do have some lovely timeshare vacation units to show you," Tony the facilitator said, his smile getting brighter and perkier until I thought it might actually blind me.

"Run, Emily. I will protect you. Escape while you can."

"You'll have to excuse him," I told Tony as he stopped before us, his hand out. Brother stood in front of me with his hands held out at his sides, like he was trying to block Tony from getting to me. I pushed down Brother's arm and shook Tony's hand. "He's just had a birthday last month, and he's still trying to recover from the shock of finding out he's officially elderly."

"Fifty-two is not elderly," Brother said, yanking me back when I was going to go to the table Tony waved us toward. "Emily, I forbid you to sit down. I've heard all about these places. They brainwash you into buying time in condos you don't want or need. Once you sit down you're a goner. I heard they put something in the air, some drug to make you compliant and mindless. Come along now. Let's leave while we still have our brains."

"It's too late for some of us," I muttered, but stopped and frowned at Tony.

"I assure you, Mr. Williams, there is no force or coercion used at all by Vacation Paradiso. The vacation units sell themselves. If you'll just have a seat here, I have a short video that will explain everything—"

"Arrrrrrrgh!" Brother yelled. "No videos! I know all about those subliminal messages you people put in them! You'll have us slaves to your evil economic powers! Run, Emily. Run as fast as you can. Save yourself."

Honestly, Holly, it was so embarrassing I thought I was going to die right there. Luckily no one else was in the office but the receptionist woman, so after a while, once I got Brother calmed down (I had to promise I'd leave if I felt the slightest urge to buy anything), I finally got to ask Tony what I wanted to ask.

"Yeah, that's a really nice condo and stuff, and Madrid looks like a really interesting city to visit," I said after he showed me pictures of some place in Spain. "But I'm just here to pick up my Extremely Valuable Prize. The prize woman said I didn't have to buy anything to get it. So can I get it, please?"

"Absolutely, I will be happy to take you back into our lotto room for you to spin the big wheel and get your Extremely Valuable Prize—one of five Extremely Valuable Prizes available—but first, let me show you some price comparisons between hotels and a condo with Vacation Paradiso. . . ."

I glanced at Brother, a little worried. We'd been there for an hour, and he'd been sitting in the chair with his eyes closed (he refused to be subliminally influenced by the vacation videos), his arms crossed, and his lips clamped shut tight. I had to watch carefully to make sure he was still breathing. Mom would never forgive me if Brother died while I was trying to get my EVP.

"OK, you know what? Let's just pretend that you showed me the prices, and I was, like, really, really amazed and stuff, and let's go get my EVP instead, so I can get my father home before he goes catatonic or something on me."

Tony smiled at me—kind of a piranha smile. It was scary, and I started worrying that maybe Brother hadn't exaggerated the situation quite as much as I originally thought. "There's nothing I'd like to do more, Emily, but if we did that, you'd miss seeing not only some very lovely videos of our many facilities around the world, but also hearing testimonials from the many thousands of satisfied members of the Vacation Paradiso family, not to mention the fabulous tour of a sample unit located right here in Seattle!"

"Er," I said, eyeing Brother. His face had gone all rigid, like rigor mortis or something like that had set in. "I don't suppose you have a mirror?"

Tony blinked at me, his smile slipping a little bit. "A mirror?"

"Yeah, or a pin or something so I can see if Brother is still alive? I'm worried he may be dead. And that's just going to be trouble, what with the coroner's inquest, and the newspaper guys coming to take pictures and interview me as to why my father died here during one of your presentations. No doubt there'll be some sort of investigation as to what could have killed him here."

"Investigation?" Tony said, his smile dissolving into nothing.

"Oh, yeah, big investigation," I said, noticing that the very corners of Brother's lips curved ever so slightly upward, like he was fighting a smile of his own. "You know how people are—if they hear about someone dying somewhere, they run away from it like mad. I had an aunt who was in real estate for a while, and she couldn't sell a house where some guy went wacko and started shooting people from his attic. I mean, who wants to live in a house where wacko brain waves could still be floating around?"

"Wacko brain waves?" he repeated, his eyes flitting between Brother and me. I swear to God, Holly— Brother looked positively dead sitting there next to me. Tony licked his lips nervously and cleared his throat.

"It's a karma thing," I told him. "You know, like a person's essence remaining behind to haunt a place where they are killed? People get freaky about things like that."

"They do?" he asked, his voice a little squeaky. "I hadn't heard about that."

"Oh, yeah, I'm very hip to the paranormal stuff," I said. "I have an underwear-drawer ghost, although lately he's branching out beyond undies. Well, if you don't have a mirror, maybe I'll just run to the bathroom and freshen up so when the newspaper photographers come to take my picture next to my dead father, I'll look good. And what was your full name again? I'll want to be sure I get it right when I talk to the reporters."

"Reporters?" he said on a horrified gasp.

I leaned over toward Brother and put my hand in front of his mouth. "I don't think he's breathing. . . ."

"Er . . . as your father is unwell, I think we can waive the rest of the presentation. If you need assistance getting him out to your car, I will be happy to help."

I smiled my brightest smile, the one where I show all my teeth. "Thank you. But first, the Extremely Valuable Prize?"

"Eh . . ." he started to say.

I put my hand on Brother's neck, right below his jaw. "Do you know where it is you feel for someone's pulse?"

"I'll get your prize voucher right now," Tony said, leaping up from his chair and bolting out of the cubicle.

I chuckled to myself as Brother cracked one eye open.

"You are a wickedly clever manipulator," he said, giving me a quick pat on the shoulder. "You get that from *my* side of the family."

Anyhoo, that's how I got the cruise. It's for a week, leaving from Seattle and going up to Alaska, which isn't at all tropical or fun-sounding, but Fang thought it was cool, and it *is* a cruise, and it will be *very romantic*, so I'm excited.

Crap, I have to run. It's late, Dru is messaging me, I still have those stupid footnotes to write on my paper, and you know how I hate footnotes. Oh, hey, how's your latest? What's his name? Bartholomew or something Harry Potterish like that? He's number six now, isn't he? You've just turned into a wild woman, yes, you have! Spill all, GF. Need details. And piccies! Send piccies!

Hugsies and all,
~Em

You have a Chat Girl Instant Message. Click to receive it.

GonnaMarryFelix: What are you doing?

Em=c^2: Writing to Holly. What are you doing?

GonnaMarryFelix: Picking out desserts for the rehearsal dinner. I was thinking something elegant, like a champagne sorbet.

Em=c^2: Aaaaaaaaaaaaaaaaaaaaaaaack! Dru! THERE IS NO REHEARSAL DINNER!

GonnaMarryFelix: You don't have to *yell* at me, Em!

Em=c^2: I give up. I totally give up. You're lost to us, sucked into the nefarious Bride World. I just hope my next best friend is a lesbian.

GonnaMarryFelix: Nefarious?

Em=c^2: It was on my *Word a Day* calendar last week. I think it means creepy.

GonnaMarryFelix: Bride stuff is not creepy!

Em=c^2: Uh-huh.

Em=c^2: Let me just ask you this—which one of us, at this very moment, is living in La-La Land?

GonnaMarryFelix: I'm *so* not going to talk to you when you're in this mood.

Em=c^2: !!!

GonnaMarryFelix: Did you do your footnotes?

Em=c^2: Of course not. They are evil and must be ignored until the last minute.

GonnaMarryFelix: That's my plan, too.

Em=c^2: So . . . ?

GonnaMarryFelix: What?

Em=c^2: You know, there's a lot to be said for being a lesbian. You can wear your girlfriend's clothes, and she

42

would go shopping with you without making a face or making you go look at tires and stuff at Sears, and she would understand cramps.

GonnaMarryFelix: I am not going to become a lesbian! I love Felix!

Em=c^2: You should think about it. I think it would be good for you. It would open up new horizons and stuff, and you're always going on about New Age things like that.

GonnaMarryFelix: I

GonnaMarryFelix: AM

GonnaMarryFelix: NOT GOING TO BECOME A LESBIAN!

Em=c^2: I never knew you were whatchamacallit . . . lesbianphobic.

GonnaMarryFelix: I am not homophobic! I like gay people! My uncle is gay! I'm totally supportive of gay rights! I just don't like girls that way!

Em=c^2: You're not thinking this through, Dru. Look at it this way—if you were a lesbian, you'd talk all the time to your girlfriend. You'd share her clothes, and borrow her perfume, and help her pick out underwear and stuff. *Just the sort of thing we do together!* So see, you're partway there!

GonnaMarryFelix: I don't like you well enough for that!

Em=c^2: /me gasps!

GonnaMarryFelix: You know what I mean!

Em=c^2: There's nothing to be ashamed of in having lesbian feelings, Dru. Everyone has them. Well, not me, but I'm in love with Fang. But other girls do, and it's OK. In fact, I think it's kind of cool. I mean, it's very chic right now.

GonnaMarryFelix: You're totally insane, you know that? I can't think of anyone else who would try to talk me into being gay just because she didn't want to help me plan the most beautiful wedding that will ever be.

Em=c^2: It's not working?

GonnaMarryFelix: No.

Em=c^2: You don't want to, like . . . kiss me or anything?

GonnaMarryFelix: No!

Em=c^2: . . .

Em=c^2: I think you're repressing your true inner emo—

Your Chat Girl friend GonnaMarryFelix has logged off.

Em=c^2: Dru? *sigh*

Subject: re: What do you mean, he kissed you?
From: Emster@seattlegrrl.com
To: Fbaxter@doormouse.ca
Date: June 16, 2005 7:34 pm
>

There's not something you need to tell me?

Silly Fang. As if there is anyone in the whole, entire world—and that includes Orlando and Billy and Johnny D—who makes me go all melty like you do. Devon just kissed me hello. A friendly, nonsexy, former-BF-but-no-longer-on-the-BF-list kiss. It was absolutely nothing. Well, OK, it was nice, but that's because it was Devon, and all the other stuff that followed didn't mean anything, either.

Two days until grad weekend! I can't wait to see you!

Major kissies!
Emily

Subject: re: Absolutely nothing?
From: Emster@seattlegrrl.com
To: Fbaxter@doormouse.ca
Date: June 16, 2005 7:39 pm
>
> *What do you mean, it was nice because it was De-*
> *von? What other stuff followed? Just*
> *what exactly happened?*

Nothing! Nothing happened! Nothing at all! He just kissed me hello, and then we went to the hospital, and later we sat in bed together all night. But I had my clothes on the whole time. So see? Nothing.

Love you!
Em

Subject: re: EMILY!
From: Emster@seattlegrrl.com
To: Fbaxter@doormouse.ca
Date: June 16, 2005 7:39 pm

> *doing this on purpose, aren't you? WHAT HAP-*
> *PENED?*

Sigh. All right, since you're going to make such a big thing about it, I'll tell you. But I want credit for the fact that the only reason I told you in the first place is because I don't ever want you thinking I'm keeping things from you. I would never do that, Fang. I want you to know that I'll always tell you everything, because I know you'll understand.

OK, here's what happened—I got Brother to pick Devon up at the airport. That wasn't easy, since I had to promise him I'd never make him dance with me in the hallway again, but whatever. I was just printing out my stupid cold war paper when Brother and Devon pulled up.

"Devon's here," I yelled to Mom as I charged out of my bedroom. "Are all the freaky naked pictures put away?"

"My nudes are not freaky," Mom said, wiping her hands on a dish towel as she came out of the kitchen. "I hope Devon likes eggplant. Did you ask him if he had any food allergies?"

"You can ask him," I said, running to the front door

and throwing it open. Devon was just getting out of Brother's car. I got all excited because it was Devon! I mean, not *excited* excited, but happy excited, because he is my best guy friend next to you, and I haven't seen him in almost a year. So I screamed *"Devon!"* and leaped down the stairs to the driveway.

"Emily!" he yelled back, and opened his arms up wide. I screamed again and threw myself down the stairs toward him, almost as happy as I am when I see you, but not quite.

"Argh!" we both said as I tripped on the last step and went flying into him, knocking him to the side and sending him slamming into the big brick planter next to the garage door.

"*Omigod!* Devon! Are you all right?"

"Dear God!" Mom yelled from the doorway, and rushed out to see how badly Devon was hurt. "Don't move! Did you hit your head? Emily, go call nine-one-one."

"I'm all right. I think," Devon said, trying to sit up. I knelt next to him, my heart in my throat as he turned to face me. "No need for concern."

"Blood!" I yelled, my stomach doing all sorts of icky things as blood seeped out of a gash on Devon's forehead. "He's bleeding! *Omigod!*"

"It's all right," Devon said again, touching his forehead. He flinched like it really hurt.

"Are you sure? You could have a neck injury," Mom said as she got to us.

Brother was at the back of the car, hauling Devon's luggage out of the trunk. He dropped Devon's bags on the ground and gave me a narrow-eyed look.

"Well, I see Emily has greeted you in typical fashion. Let's see how badly she's damaged you."

"I didn't damage him!" I protested as Brother pushed me out of the way to look at Devon's head. By then his entire face and shirt were coated with blood, and he had blood on his hands, and I had it on my hands from where I was trying to help him.

Brother shot me a look.

"OK, I did, but it was an accident! I tripped!"

"It wasn't Emily's fault," Devon agreed, wincing when Brother turned his head to get a better look at Devon's forehead.

"See? Is he all right?" I asked, wringing my hands. Yeah, I know, it sounds weird, but I actually was standing there wringing my hands.

"I'll take him to the hospital," Brother said, sighing as he helped Devon up.

Devon started protesting that he was fine (I wrung my hands even more at that, because there was *so much blood!*), but Brother and Mom overruled him, and in the end we all went to the hospital.

They didn't even put in any stitches, although they did have to pick out all sorts of dirt and stuff from the owie, which was really gross. The hospital guy said we had to watch for signs of a concussion, like if Devon got really sleepy or felt sick to his stomach, so I told Devon that because it was my fault he was hurt, I'd do the nurse thing and watch over him to make sure his brain didn't explode, or whatever it does when you get a concussion and things go badly.

"Em—you don't have to sit up with me. I'm quite all right," Devon said a couple of hours later, as everyone was getting ready to go to bed.

"Of course I do. I wounded you! It's my duty. Get your jammies on, and I'll be right back. I just have to get a few things to help me through the long, dark hours of the night."

"I don't wear anything to bed," he said with a totally Devon grin. (You know, the one where his eyes sparkle and everything . . . not that I noticed. And his eyes aren't nearly as nice as yours. I like yours much better. And your smile—you have a smile that makes me go all quivery inside, whereas Devon's smile just makes me want to smile back. But a quivery smile is much, much better than a smiley smile. Where was I? Oh, yeah . . .)

"Oh," I said, and thought about asking him to wear PJs this once, but then I decided I wouldn't. I am eighteen and all, and he's my best guy friend next to you, and I've barfed on him twice and now given him a concussion, so it's not like I don't know him. If he wanted to be naked while I was in the same room, I was totally cool with that. I mean, I didn't care at all. It was a noncaring thing. You know what I mean? "OK. Be right back."

By the time I got into my nonsexy jammies (I wouldn't

wear sexy around anyone but you *blows kiss*), grabbed my bottle of diet Coke, my books, my MP3 player, my Johnny Depp deck of cards, my laptop, a couple of bottles of nail polish (I wanted to do some really cool striped nails in school colors for grad weekend, and I needed to practice my stripes), and some nachos in case Devon was hungry, and went back to the spare bedroom, he was sitting in bed, his chest all bare and stuff, but blankets around all the really important parts.

Not, you understand, that I cared one single bit for his important parts.

"Is that all for me?" he asked as I plopped everything down onto the chair and dragged it over to the bed. "Good Lord, is there anything left in your bedroom?"

"Nope, it's not all for you, and ha, ha, ha. You can have some nachos, if you want. Is Coke all right? Or do you want something nonfizzy? We have chai, too."

"Coke is fine, although I don't normally eat and drink in bed. What are you doing?" he asked as I pushed the blankets up against his side.

"Trying to shove you over. Thanks. I'll just sit here and read and stuff while you sleep," I said, plopping down when he scooted over on the bed. I fluffed a pillow up behind me, gave him the plate of nachos to hold, and poured a couple of glasses of Coke. "Do you want to play some cards first, before you go to sleep? I can just read and do stripy nails if you're sleepy."

He started laughing. I got a little worried about him

because he laughed so hard he spilled the nachos every-where, and then he started to get up to pick them off the bedspread, but I figured you wouldn't want me to see Devon naked, even though he's not my BF or any-thing. So I cleaned it up and made him stay in bed, and it just happened that we spent most of the night talking and playing cards, and eating and doing our nails and stuff. (Devon let me practice stripes on his fingernails, but made me take it off when I was done.)

So, you see? Nothing important happened.

I can't wait to see you on Saturday. Devon is going to come up with us to B.C.; then he'll take off and visit some girl he met online. I think he mentioned her to you? Her name is Saliva or something really, really weird like that. I just bet you she's Gother than Goth. Anyway, I told him he could spend the weekend with us, but he said that since he'll be seeing you in a few days anyway, he won't cramp our style. Isn't that sweet of him?

Big fat kissies!
Emily

Subject: re: Sorry, Em
From: Emster@seattlegrrl.com
To: Fbaxter@doormouse.ca
Date: June 17, 2005 3:55 pm
>
> *I'm sorry to disappoint you, but I feel like the arse end*

> of a dead goat. I'm running a fever, and I can't keep
> anything down. I know you planned all sorts of won-
> derful things for us this weekend, but I'm not going
> to be able to make it. I don't want to give you this
> virus. One of us being miserable is enough.

One of us? One of us!!! Try two, Fang! Oh, crod, I have to leave, or we'll miss the train to Vancouver. Are you sure you couldn't just come to town to see me for the weekend? We wouldn't have to do anything strenuous. We could just sit around and look at things, and maybe see a movie or something.

Sigh. Ignore that. I'm being selfish and inconsiderate. If you're sick, stay in bed and get better (you have to be well for the cruise!). I'm disappointed, of course, but I'll survive the weekend. *Somehow.*

Hugsies and lots of warm fuzzies to make you better. I'll call you from Vancouver, OK?

Sad, but completely supportive because your health matters more than my happiness,
Emily

Subject: Re: How was your grad weekend?
From: Emster@seattlegrrl.com
To: Hollyberry@britsahoy.co.uk
Date: June 20, 2005 4:09 pm
> *Did you have lots of fun seeing Fang?*

Ik dindntsee him.,

eM

Subject: Re: Are you OK?
From: Emster@seattlegrrl.com
To: Hollyberry@britsahoy.co.uk
Date: June 21, 2005 7:18 pm

> *Emily? Is something wrong? You typoed all over the*
> *place, and that's not at all like you. Are you crying? Is*
> *something going on with you and Fang? Oh, please*
> *tell me you two haven't broken up. You're so right*
> *together!*

Sigh.
Siiiiiiiiiiiiiigh.
No, seriously, sigh^3.
Today was graduation. I am now officially a high school graduate. Yay. I am also typing this e-mail with one hand, and it's taking me for-fricking-ever. Sorry about the typos in the e-mail yesterday—I was kind of wonked out on pain meds, and that was my first time trying to type with one hand.

First things first—Fang and I are just fine. I think. I don't know that absolutely for certain, because I didn't get to see him this weekend. I did call him before the horrible event that ruined my life, but only for a couple of minutes, because he couldn't really talk. Evidently the flu or cold or whatever it is has gone into his throat. But he grunted at me, and it sounded like romantic 'I-miss-you' grunts, so I think all is well there. I'm going to look up glandular fever on Google, though. I think Fang grunted something about it—that or he was saying good-bye. I'm not exactly sure which.

The grad weekend started out bleh. With Fang sick, it meant I'd have to hang out with the rest of the seniors who went to Vancouver, and not have a wonderfully romantic getaway with the nummiest BF on earth. Naturally, I was disappointed.

"You still pouting?" Dru asked as we got off the train in downtown Vancouver. (It's kind of like Seattle, but Canadian, if you know what I mean. People there say "Eh?" a lot. They also really like doughnuts. And their hospitals . . . well, I'll get to that.)

"I'm not pouting. I never pout. I am the antithesis of pouting," I said with a whole lot of dignity and stuff.

She frowned. "Antithesis?"

"I am *so* getting you a *Word a Day* calendar for Christmas," I told her. "It means . . . um . . . basically it means that Emily does not pout."

"Uh-huh. So refusing to talk to anyone all the way up here wasn't pouting? OK. Whatever. Do you want to go to the park, the aquarium, or shopping in Gastown? I vote shopping. I bet they have really cool Canadian bridal wear here."

I ignored the bridal mention, because I have decided

that if she can ignore the fact that Felix is in the army for four years, and won't be back in the U.S. for at least two of those four years, then I can ignore the fact that she's insane. "I don't care. It's all the same to me now that my life is over."

She rolled her eyes, just like I knew she would, and we took off. Technically we were all supposed to stick together for grad weekend, but no one paid any attention to that, and everyone pretty much split up and went off to do what they wanted. Who wants to spend the weekend being chaperoned?

"Right, so Science World or shopping?" Dru said as we dumped our bags in the tiny hotel room we were going to share for the weekend. "I vote shopping."

"Maybe I should just call Fang," I said, looking at the phone.

"You just did, and he said he was trying to take a nap."

"I know, but he sounded so pathetic. Like a frog who had swallowed a bunch of gravel or something. Maybe I should take the train out to Barlbury and check on him."

"And get his cold?" Dru whapped me on the arm. "Come on, let's go. This is our big weekend! We're free! Monday is graduation! Let's go buy things."

"But . . . Fang!"

"Will be all right," she said, forcibly dragging me out of the room and away from the phone. "He told you that himself. He just needs to rest and stuff like that. C'mon, c'mon, c'mon! I've got money! Buy stuff!"

In the end, we decided to go to Science World—a

very cool science museum complex that has an OMNI-MAX theater (they show movies on the curved dome of the ceiling rather than a normal IMAX big screen).

"The only reason I'm doing this is because you're looking so pathetic," Dru said as we left the hotel and headed for the waterfront Skytrain station.

"Uh huh. And the fact that there's a Stomp movie at the OMNIMAX doesn't come into it at all, right?"

Did I tell you that Dru has a girl-crush (not sexual or anything like that) on a flamenco dancer named Eva Yerbabuena? She's a Spanish dancer. Really good and all that, but all Dru has had is two years of dance, and she's *not* very good. But whatever—it's good for her to have a non–fantasy wedding obsession. Anyway, this Eva flamenco chick is in the Stomp movie.

"I don't know what you're blathering about," Dru said, using her very best English voice.

"You know, that really ticks me off," I said as we dashed across the street for the Skytrain station. I waved at a car that honked at us.

"What?" she asked. "That I told you to stop blathering?"

"No, that you can do an English accent better than me. I lived there for a whole year, and you were only there for a couple of days, but you sound all Emma Thompson, while I sound like the woman who plays Drusilla on *Buffy*."

"Her accent is *so* bad," Dru said, looking pleased. We hurried into the waterfront train station, yelling hi to a couple of classmates who were in there hitting up a food place.

"Uh-huh. Which train do we want?" I said, stopping at a machine that gave you tickets if you fed it money.

Dru consulted the Vancouver guidebook we'd bought at the hotel. "Um . . . says the main station."

"Gotcha." I inserted a couple of loonies (the Canadian dollar coins—they have loons on one side, so they're called loonies. They also have two-dollar coins that are called toonies, although they don't have cartoons on them) and grabbed the tickets. I looked at the schedule board and did a little scream. "Train leaving *right now!*"

"Eeek!" Dru screamed. We bolted for the platform.

Now, here's the thing about the waterfront train station—it *looks* like a normal train station. Big area with shops and stuff, then the train part with long platforms and trains. The thing is, it's not normal—it's the train station from hell! They have special super slippery floors to catch unwary American visitors whose names start with the letter E as they are running for a train.

"Don't let them go," I yelled to Dru, who has swimmer's legs and all and can run faster than me. She dashed toward the train, which was just revving up to leave. I tried for a Spiderman-like leap for the train, but the floors—from hell, remember?—did a weird slipping thing beneath me, and I ended up flat on my face.

"Are you all right?" a lady asked as I lay there, my face smashed into the evil cement floor. For a second or two all I could think of was how embarrassing stuff always seems to be happening to me, then I tried to push myself up and the pain hit.

"Argh!" I yelled, rolling over onto my back and clutching my hand. My right hand. You know, the shake part of the shake-and-take-the-diploma thing.

People from the other side of the platform came over to see me. Dru pushed her way through them, calling my name. "Emily? What happened? Why are you rolling around on the ground? Omicrod, what's wrong with your hand?"

"Looks broken to me," the woman who was now trying to help me up said. I got to my feet, swaying as huge waves of pain radiated up from my poor little hand. I looked down at it. It didn't look right. It wasn't all bent backward or anything gross like that, but it didn't look right. "You'd best go to the hospital and have them take a look at it."

"Let's get a paramedic or something," Dru said.

A couple of people around her nodded. One pulled out a cell phone.

"No!" I shouted, then smiled at all the people. It hurt to smile, not because my face was smashed or anything, but by that point everything on my body hurt. There was a limit to the amount of humiliation I could take, and paramedics were out. I knew from our time at the castle in Scotland just how much attention you get from everyone with paramedics around. "I'm OK, really. See? Just sprained or something."

"You really should have that seen to," First Woman repeated, brushing me down a little. Thank God I was in jeans and not a skirt, where everyone could see my undies and stuff.

"Yeah, but no paramedics."

"Em . . ." Dru frowned at me, but I gave her Eyebrows of Much Meaning, and she shut up. Someone told us which bus to take to get to the hospital, and after I glared at the Demon Floor of Extreme Evilness, Dru and I left the train station and went to find the bus.

Crap. Be right back. Gotta do the dinner thing. I'd eat by myself but I have to have someone cut up my food.

Sigh.
~Em

Subject: My life—you can have it
From: Emster@seattlegrrl.com
To: Hollyberry@britsahoy.co.uk
Date: June 21, 2005 7:55 pm

I'm back. You want to know what humiliation feels like? Try having to have your mom cut up your food in front of professors from the same office where your father works. Brother had a couple of profs and their husbands over for dinner to talk about his book, and horror of all horrors, Mom actually said as she handed me my plate, "I'll cut that chicken up into tiny little pieces for you, dear."

I'd say, "Kill me now," but I have Fang, and now I'm a grad, so I don't really want to die. But almost.

Back to the weekend. It took us a while (seemed like forever to me, but the pain from my hand was making my brain weird), but we finally found the bus and got on it, telling the driver we wanted to go to the hospital. We sat in the back so no one would bounce around next to me. I thought seriously about crying, but you know that I just get gross when I cry, what with the nose-stuffing-up thing, and blotchy red skin, and puffy eyes, and all. So I scrapped that plan and went straight to hard-core whining.

"Why me? Why, why, why me?" I asked Dru, cradling my poor, damaged hand to my chest.

"Could be karma," Dru said calmly, turning to give me a long look before going back to scanning the shops for bridal stores.

"Karma? Like, I'm being punished for doing something bad?" I asked, kinda shocked.

"Yeah. Bhagwan Vainra says that the karma payback always works, and if bad things are happening to you, it means that you're doing something to harm someone, and you'd better shape up before karma really gets pissed at you."

"Bad things? I don't do bad things to people," I protested, shocked and all that she'd even think that. "I'm good! I don't eat mammals, and I spend one weekend a month tutoring at the women's shelter, and I willingly gave up Chinese fireworks because of the unsafe work conditions the fireworks guys had to put up with. I'm good! Karma just has it in for me, that's all, and I'm getting sick and tired of it."

"You know," Dru said thoughtfully, twirling her hair around her finger like she always does when she thinks hard, "my cousin Mandy broke her hand once."

"What does that have to do with karma?"

She gave me a look. "Nothing. I'm not going to talk to you about karma because you are an unbeliever."

It was my turn to roll my eyes. Ever since Dru went to a holistic place to have a wart taken off her toe, she's been all New Agey. I blame the Vainra guy who runs the place. He's really flaky, and always makes me feel like I need to take a shower after I've been in the shop. "I'm a physicist in training. We are natural skeptics because we know how stuff works, rather than just guessing about things."

"Not going there," Dru said (I'd won the last three out of five arguments we'd had about all the weird stuff that Bhagwan Vainra tells her). "Anyway, my cousin Mandy broke her hand, and they ended up doing a spinal on her."

"A what?" I squawked (not proud of it, but I'm honest, if nothing else). A couple of people in the bus turned back to look at us.

"A spinal tap. You know, where they drill a hole into your spine and suck fluids out of it? Mandy said it hurt so bad she wanted to set her hair on fire. She screamed and screamed and screamed, but no one would stop, and they didn't give her pain pills or anything. It hurt so bad she barfed all over the hospital table, but even then they wouldn't stop, and made her lay in it, screaming and crying and begging them to stop, until they were done."

"La vache," I said, my stomach turning inside out on itself. I swear, Holly, the hair on my arms stood on end. "Why would they do a spinal on her for a broken hand?"

Dru shrugged. "I never did find out. Every time I mention it to Mandy she starts crying. I think it had something to do with whether or not she had nerve damage in her broken hand. You know, all the nerves go back to the spine."

"Omigod," I said, starting to hyperventilate a little at the thought. "Well, I don't care what the guys at this hospital think—I'm not going to let them do a spinal on me!"

"It's probably best if you don't," Dru said, then looked back out the window. "Mandy didn't walk right for three months afterward."

I didn't say anything for the rest of the bus ride to the hospital, but I did make a solemn promise to myself that I would be assertive and proactive and all that stuff from when I was reclaiming Fang from Audrey. (I got an e-mail from her the other day, BTW—she said to say hi to you.) No one was going to touch my spine!

By the time we got off the bus, my hand was swollen up like a melon, my whole body hurt, and all I could think about was what horrible pain a spinal would be on top of everything else.

"Hi, I'm Dru," Dru said to the hospital emergency room woman. "This is Emily. She broke her hand. We're American, and we're here having our grad weekend."

"I see," the hospital lady said, frowning at my hand. "Do you have travel health insurance?"

Dru looked at me.

"Um," I said, holding up my hand. "You know, this really hurts. Ow. See? Just moving it makes my head throb."

"I understand that, but before we can see you, we need to get information about your health insurance."

"Oh. Well, there was something we had to pay fifty bucks for when we signed up for the weekend. I think that was insurance."

"Do you have your insurance card?" Hospital Woman said, tapping something into the computer in front of her.

I looked at Dru again. "Do you have one?"

"No. I don't think I got one. What about you?"

"All I have is a broken hand," I said, starting to cry.

"Look, she's crying! Are you happy now?" Dru told Hospital Woman.

"Hospital policy—" the woman started to say.

"I always thought Canadians were nice," Dru interrupted, getting all mad and stuff. I wanted to hug her, but didn't because my hand was hurting so much, I wanted to barf. "But you're just mean to make poor Em cry! Can't you just, like, set her hand and then figure out the insurance stuff?"

"Hospital policy is that we must have information about insurance or an alternate means of payment before we can treat the patient," the (now evil) woman said, "but we are forbidden by law to turn anyone away because of lack of insurance. We prefer payment, however."

"I have my mom's Visa," I said, sniffling a lot because it's just sooo lame to stand in an emergency room and cry right out in the open where everyone can see you.

"Are you an authorized user?" HW asked, her eyes all suspicious.

"Well, yeah!"

She perked up at that, and before you could say, "No spinal taps!" the woman took all my info, typed in mom's Visa card number, put a plastic band around my good wrist, and told me to go back to bay five, where a nurse would take care of me.

Dru started to follow behind me, but HW stopped her. "Are you family?"

"Well . . . I'm her best friend since we were two. That's like family, isn't it?" Dru answered. I nodded, feeling sicker by every second.

"I'm sorry; only family is allowed into the emergency room. You'll have to wait out here."

Dru shot me an agonized look. I knew she was doing her best, but I didn't have the energy to either thank her or help her. "But her family is in Seattle!"

"Only family is allowed," HW said, pointing to a waiting area. "You can wait there."

"Oh, Em," Dru said, looking like she wanted to cry for me.

"It's OK," I said, having to blink really fast so I didn't start crying again. "I'll be all right."

Dru moved close to me so no one could hear her. "Don't worry; I'm not going to leave you alone. I'll wait until she isn't looking, then sneak in."

We both looked at Hospital Woman. She narrowed her eyes at us.

"I would feel better with you there," I admitted. "But I don't want you getting into trouble or anything."

"You'd do the same for me," she said, giving me a little hug.

"Yeah, but how are you going to do it? That woman is watching us like a hawk."

"I'll Lucy my way in," Dru said, giving me a secretive smile.

"Lucy? Lucy who? Oh, no, wait. You don't mean the *I Love Lucy* Lucy?"

"Of course," Dru said, still smiling. If I had been feeling better, I would have rolled my eyes. "Lucy can teach us much. Bhagwan Vainra has this book called *The Tao of Lucy,* and it has lots of examples how we can apply Lucy's teachings to our everyday lives."

"Oh, man," I said, wanting to laugh and cry at the same time.

"I'll be in as soon as I can."

There wasn't anything I could do. I really didn't want to wait by myself, so I nodded and went into the emergency area, giving the nurse in charge my chart. She was really nice, and *tsk*ed over my owie hand, taking me back to a little bay that was separated from the others by long curtains on a U-shaped track that ran around the fringes of the bay. She took my blood pressure, asked questions about how I'd hurt my hand, and told me it would be just a few minutes before someone came to take me to X-ray.

"Um. I don't know what your hospital policy is about spinal taps for hand injuries, but I'd like to say right here and now that I don't want one. I'm sure I don't have any nerve damage, so it's absolutely not necessary."

The woman looked at me as if I had a spinal cord on my head.

"All right," she finally said.

"It would be a waste of insurance money and stuff to do one," I pointed out, because Brother says doctors and nurses always are nicer to you if you are considerate of their work environment. Thank God I had to do a report last fall on how health insurance works. "And lower insurance costs mean higher benefits for everyone."

"Indeed."

"So it'll save everyone just buckets of money if we don't go the expensive and unnecessary spinal-test route, and stick to a simple X-ray," I added.

She took a deep breath, opened her mouth to say

something, but closed it and shook her head.

"Could you write 'No spinal tap' on my chart, please?" I asked, figuring it was better to have it written down where everyone could see it.

"I'll see what I can do," she said, setting the chart in a little slot just outside the bay.

I frowned as she closed the curtains behind her. I was left alone in the bay, all alone, just me and my big fat swollen hand, which was now approximately the size of a watermelon. I lay down on the crinkly paper-covered bed, but that was too uncomfortable, so I ended up reading all the horrible notices on the wall about how to stop someone from choking, and how to hook up an EKG unit, and just what genital warts could do to you (don't ask—it's too icky for words).

Just as I was about to peek through the curtains and see where the nurse went to, they rippled a little and someone's eye peered in for a second.

"There you are," Dru said as she slipped into the bay. "I thought you were in the one down farther, but that was an old man who didn't have his shirt on. He coughed a lot. Have they said anything about a spinal tap?"

"No, thank God, but the nurse wouldn't write on my chart that I didn't want one." I was getting a little weepy again that Dru was there for me. I don't know why it made it better having her there, but it did. Now if anyone tried to spinal tap me, she could run out and get help.

"She didn't? Oooh." Dru frowned. "That's a bad sign, don't you think?"

"Well . . . you think it's bad? I thought maybe it was because she hadn't planned on doing one."

"That could be. But it could also be that they just don't want you screaming and yelling and stuff, like Mandy did. There are other patients here, and they'd probably be upset if you were yelling your head off."

"Eeek," I said, jumping off the paper-covered table so I could pace the tiny little bay. "What am I going to do?"

"Where's the chart?"

"Outside the room," I said miserably, certain now that the nurse was off rounding up the spinal-tap team. "Why did I have to come to Canada? This whole trip has been nothing but awful! Dru, promise me if I die from pain overdose, you'll help Brother sue the crap out of this hospital."

"Promise, but it won't be necessary," she said as she parted the curtains about an inch and peered out. Before I could ask what she was doing she disappeared, popping back into the bay almost instantly, my chart in her hands. "Right, we'll just make a big old note right here at the bottom. . . ."

"Oh, Dru, thank you," I said, getting sniffly again. "Just for that, you can talk wedding for a whole half hour and I won't once make gacking noises."

She smiled at me as she showed me the big NO SPINAL TAP written on the chart. She had written it in blue ink, then gone back over it with a yellow highlighter so it really stood out. "Deal. On the way home I'll tell you about this fabulous New Year's Eve wedding I read about."

A few minutes after she slipped the chart back, a guy came for me with a wheelchair, telling me he was the orderly who would take me to X-ray. I made him promise he wasn't taking me to the spinal tap room before I'd get into the chair. Dru waited in the room while they took piccies of my hand from all sorts of angles (which hurt *a lot,* let me tell you!), and when the orderly (not cute at all) dropped me back off in my bay, Dru was chatting up a really hot looking doctor. Think Doogie Howser, only cuter. More like Toby McGuire, only with lighter hair.

"Ah, this must be our hurt visitor," the doctor said. He smiled at me, and despite the pain of my hand I smiled back, because it just doesn't pay to not smile at hotties. "I'm Dr. Grant, Miss Williams. Your sister was just telling me about her fiancé."

Sister. Hee. I couldn't look at Dru or else I'd giggle, so I just kept my eyes on the handsome Dr. Grant (which wasn't really a problem,'cause he was *hot* with a capital H! And O and T, too!) and smiled a lot. Not my special Fang smile, because it would be wrong to smile that way at another guy, but a really nice smile. A Devon-grade smile. "Hi. Yeah, I'm Emily."

"I'm glad to hear that. Now, let me just look at your details while we wait for the X-rays to be processed. . . . Ah. I see we're *not* going to be doing a spinal tap today."

"No, I've decided to pass on that option," I said, trying to look responsible and all that. "I'm really sure there's not nerve damage or anything, so there's no need to waste anyone's money or time doing one."

"How very thoughtful of you. I wish all our patients had half as much foresight as you," he said, coming over to me. "Now, let me take a look at your hand. Ow. I bet that hurts."

"Like hell," I said, then made big eyes. "Oh, sorry, didn't mean to have a potty mouth in front of you."

"I don't consider the word *hell* quite at the potty-mouth level, but thank you for the concern about sullying my delicate ears," he said. I looked at him carefully to see if he was ragging me, but he looked really serious, although the corners of his mouth twitched a couple of times. "Can you move your fingers?"

"I don't want to try," I said, hating that I sounded so pathetic, but really and truly sure that if I tried, my hand would hurt so much I'd barf all over him, and as you know, the only guy I barf on is Devon.

"Then don't. Oh, the X-rays. Thank you, Herve. Hmm." He slid them into an X-ray viewing thingie on the wall and turned on the lamp. I have to admit, it was very cool to see my hand bones and stuff. "Ah, yes. See here? You have fractures in your second, third, and fourth proximal phalanx bones."

"Uh," I said, squinting at the X-ray. Dru stood next to me, squinting as well.

He pointed to three spots on one of the pictures. "You did a very nice job breaking three fingers. I'm assuming your hand must have been bent under you when you fell, cracking the bones in the fingers that took the brunt of your weight. Well, I'm afraid a cast is going to be in order, but we'll try to make it a small one so as not to interfere with your graduation."

Evidently Dru had been yakking a lot while I was gone getting X-rays. Honestly, I don't know anyone who talks as much as she does.

"You'll be limiting your handshaking for a while, but you should have no permanent disability," he said as he opened the curtains and beckoned in a nurse.

"And no spinal tap," I said, just to make sure.

"Well . . ." he said, pursing his lips as he looked at my hand.

My stomach turned over. I held my breath, afraid that if I moved, I'd spew all over him.

"I guess we can let you go without one this time," he finally said, the corners of his eyes crinkling as he smiled at me. I let out my breath and held up my hand so he and the nurse could do the cast thing on it, smiling over their shoulders at Dru, who was giving me the thumbs-up sign.

The rest of the weekend pretty much sucked. My hand hurt so bad that the doctor gave me a prescription for pain meds, which just put me to sleep. So I slept most of the weekend while Dru went out with the others. I didn't get to see Fang once, and Devon disappeared until it was time to go home.

Oh, the train ride home sucked, too. Turns out there

is something metal in the cast. (It's kind of a brace more than a plaster cast, with this big elasticky bandage that wraps around my fingers, with a plaster-and-metal thing on the bottom side that keeps everything firm. I didn't think anything about it, but man, those metal detectors they have at customs really are sensitive.) Thank God I was so wonked out on pain meds that I didn't even once think about body searches, which Dru says she was worried about the instant the security guys came to get me and drag me out of the customs line because when I walked through their metal detector it had a hissy fit.

Anyhoo, that's why I was typing so weird yesterday. Graduation was . . . Well, that's going to have to wait. My fingers are starting to get sore, so I'd better go.

But before I do, what's up with you, chicky? You haven't told me anything about the new Mr. Holly. He's a sixth former, right? Is he in many of your classes? Tell!

Hugs and one-handed kisses,
~Em

You have a Chat Girl Instant Message. Click to receive it.

GonnaMarryFelix: I found the most adorable flower-girl baskets!
Em=c^2: Aaaaaaaaaargh!

*You have left Chat Girl Instant Messaging Service.
Click to restart the program.*

Subject: Yay!
From: Emster@seattlegrrl.com
To: Fbaxter@doormouse.ca
Date: June 22, 2005 9:18 am

> *How did your graduation go? I wish I could have*
> *been there, but I'm still battling this bug. I also wish*
> *you'd have called me when you broke your hand. I*
> *could have made it into Vancouver to help you. I hate*
> *the thought of you being worried and frightened.*
> *And . . . erm . . . Em? They don't do spinal taps for a*
> *broken hand.*

Yeah, that's what Brother says, too, but you know, I swear they were going to do one. That emergency room nurse woman was clearly planning on it until we scotched her little plan by writing on my chart.

Anyhoo, graduation. Eh. It was . . . um . . . you know how some people always seem to have disasters and stuff happen to them? Well, I've never been a disaster sort of person, but I have to admit that the last few days have made me wonder if someone put a curse or something on me.

It wasn't really my fault, either. The really nice doctor in Vancouver gave me some purple pain pills, and wow, do they work! They also made me a bit loopy, but I didn't realize that at the time because I was too busy being all happy and glowy and having this really, really floaty feeling. I mean, how am I supposed to know I'm drugged out if no one tells me?

Sorry, little delay there. Bess stopped by the house to laugh at me. If I wasn't worried she'd put some sort of evil all-my-hair-will-fall-out spell on me, I'd whomp her with my cast. Hey! I wonder if maybe she is the one who cursed me? She says she doesn't do any sort of black magic, but I just bet you the dark side seduced her! I'll have to ask the leader of her local Wiccan group if there's some sort of test they can do for evil to see if she's been doing mean things to me.

Back to graduation. It went pretty much the way it was supposed to go until we were all gathered, waiting to file into the gym for commencement. Dru and I and Suky (you haven't met her—she's an old friend of ours, but she's thinking about becoming a rabbi, so she hasn't been around much) were all crammed together in a locker room waiting for all the 'rents and families to sit down so we could file in and get the shindig going.

"Show me again," Dru said, narrowing her eyes at me.

"I'm sorry, my hand is broken," I said, pretending she was the local TV weather lady who used to go to school here, and who is our speaker. I waved my right hand at her and held out my left.

"Congratulations," Dru said, presenting me with a

rolled-up flyer for the Language Club. I tucked it beneath my right arm and shook her hand with my left. "That went much better. Just remember to put it beneath your right arm, not your left like you did before, or it'll fall on the floor."

"Yeah, I'll remember," I said.

"I'll bet you five bucks that Glenda Bucwater does her famous hair flip at least three times during her speech," Dru said, looking at herself for the millionth time in the mirror.

"She's not that bad," Suky said.

"Oh, yeah? It's, like, what she's known for: hair flips and making sexy eyes at the sports dude. Oh, and telling us it's going to snow when it doesn't."

"Are you all right, Em?" Suky asked, squinting at me (her glasses broke and she can't wear contacts). "You look funny."

"I don't feel very funny," I said.

Dru stopped primping to look me over. "Nervous? It's just graduation."

I shook my head. "No, although my stomach is so blechy I haven't eaten anything today. Mostly I feel bad because my hand hurts. I probably shouldn't have tried to write out all those thank-you notes for the graduation presents this afternoon, but I wanted to get them done so I can start my new life."

"Poor Em," Suky said. "Don't you have any Tylenol?"

"Yeah, I've got one pain med left, but I was saving it

for when my hand got really bad." The two of them looked at me critically. I looked back at them. "What? Do I have something hanging out of my nose? Has a pimple spontaneously erupted? Is my hair gacky?"

"You look like you're sucking on a pickle," Dru said finally. Suky nodded. "I think you should take the pill, although it'll probably make you sleepy like it did in Canada."

"That was just the train ride. All there was to do was eat and look out the window. Boring, in other words," I said, hiking up my robe so I could dig the pill out of the pocket in my skirt where I'd stuffed it, my lipstick (one cannot graduate with bare naked lips), a comb, my tiny mirror, the roll-on perfume I bought at a folk market, and the picture of you that I always carry to show people how numalicious you are.

"It wasn't boring! I was trying to tell you about the plans for my reception, but you kept falling asleep at the good parts."

I raised my eyebrows at Suky. She bobbled her head a couple times, indicating that she understood completely. She may not have been around much, what with all the rabbi stuff at her synagogue, but she had been exposed to enough of Dru that she knew just how insane poor Dru was.

I took the pill, cacked a couple of times because I tried to swallow it dry, but managed to get it down after pushing my way through the class to the drinking fountain. I was just heading back to Dru and Suky when

Mrs. Elliott (a teacher) burst into the room, looking upset. She scanned the room, found Mr. Barlind where he was yakking with a bunch of the guys (he's the guys' gym teacher, and was in charge of herding us around during commencement), and hurried over to him. The two of them talked for a minute, then they both rushed out of the room.

"Huh. Did you see that?" Dru asked when I got back to them.

"Yeah." My hand was really hurting. I was supposed to have it in a sling to keep it elevated and next to my body for protection, but the graduation gown was awful enough (ours were gold. Of all the horrible colors, gold is just the worst—it makes me look like I have leprosy), so I wasn't going to add to it by having a big blue and white sling on it, as well. I started to reconsider that, hugging my arm to my chest, wondering if it would feel better if I kept it slinged. Slung. Whatever.

"Wonder what all that was about?"

"Probably one of the parents is making a stink about Frida being the valedictorian," Dru said, pulling out her mirror again and touching up her lip gloss.

"Why would the parents care about Frida?" Suky asked.

"Because she's a Swedish foreign exchange student," Dru answered.

"Yes, but she earned the right. She had the highest GPA all year."

Dru shrugged. "Kim's dad said he was going to write

to the school board about the way they changed the requirements to be valedictorian to just look at the senior year GPA rather than all four years. She said he said it wasn't fair to us to have Euros come in and take all the honors."

"But she earned the grades," Suky argued. "She had to do the work to get them."

"I know. I like Frida! I voted for her for prom queen. I'm just telling you what Kim's dad said. Em, you starting to feel better?"

"Hmm?" I asked, blinking a couple of times. It was funny, but the voices of everyone talking around me seemed to be almost like a song sung by a choir. The words all kind of merged together like people were singing them.

"You don't look like you're sucking pickles anymore. Is the pain pill working?"

"Yeah, I think so," I said, kind of amazed at how interesting the words sounded as they left my lips. I ran my tongue around my mouth to feel if anything was different there, but it was just the usual old Emily mouth. "Wow, these pain pills work a lot better if you don't eat anything."

"You're not feeling sleepy, are you?"

I blinked a couple more times, then a couple more after that because I decided that I liked blinking. "No. Not sleepy. Just kind of . . . floaty."

"Floaty?" Dru frowned.

"Yeah. Kind of like the first time Fang told me he loved me. Happy. Floaty. And really, really good."

"Hmm," Dru said, still watching me. "OK, but I'm going to pinch you if you start to go to sleep."

"Go right ahead," I said. "I'll just stand here and listen to the music."

"Music?" Suky asked, looking around the room. "What music? There's no music playing in here, Em. What music do you hear?"

"Hmm?" I asked, but before she could sing more to me, the doors opened again and Mr. Barlind, Mrs. Elliott, and Dr. Richards came into the room.

"Attention, class!" Dr. Richards said in his bossy voice. I frowned at him because he made the pretty music stop. "There is a regrettable and very last minute change to announce. Caitlin Williks, your class salutatorian, has been in a car accident on the way to commencement."

Everyone gasped. I gasped with them, enjoying the rush of air into my lungs. I gasped a couple more times until Dru hissed at me to stop it.

"She's all right, just minor cuts and bruises, but her parents feel it's better to have her checked over at the hospital rather than attend commencement. Naturally we're all disappointed, but we wish her a swift recovery."

"He talks funny, don't you think?" I whispered to Dru. "Kind of like something from an Arnold Schwarzenegger movie."

"Shh!"

"Due to this unfortunate event, we are required to call on another student to present Caitlin's salutatory speech. Fortunately Caitlin turned in a copy of the speech for approval, so all her replacement needs to do is read it from this copy," he said, holding up a sheet of paper.

Dru turned really big eyes on me, grabbing my good arm. "Em, do you know what this means?"

"I'm thinking maybe one of those movies where Arnold tried to be funny. Those were *so* lame," I said, watching Dr. Richards and wondering if he couldn't be proof of alien life.

"Em! Listen to me! You have the third highest GPA in the class!"

"I bet he escaped from that place in New Mexico . . . Roswell," I told her.

"The salutatorian is the student with the second-highest GPA during the course of the academic year. Therefore, we turn now to the student with the third highest GPA—"

"I think I'm gonna ask him if he's ever had an autopsy done on him," I said, figuring it couldn't hurt to ask. I pushed my way between a couple of students, intending to get up close to ask him, since I figured it would embarrass him for me to bellow it out across the locker room.

"Emily Williams, please come forward. Ah, there you are. Excellent. Here is the speech. Now, you will be called up at the beginning of the ceremony. You give your speech, and introduce our guest speaker, who will present the valedictorian. Once you have given your speech, you quietly retake your seat. Is that understood?"

"Yarp," I said, then frowned because that wasn't what I meant to say. I mean, *yarp* isn't even a proper word! OK, maybe it's a word in some other language, like Inuit or Pygmy or something really rare, but I never heard *yarp* once when I was in France, and they say a whole lot of strange things there. "*La vache*," I added, just to show everyone that despite flunking the immersion course I took in Paris, I could, in fact, speak French.

"Excellent. Are we ready, Mr. Barlind? Yes? Very good. Do me proud, everyone. Do the school proud. And most of all—"

"Do the French proud?" I asked, still thinking about *yarp*.

"Er . . . do *yourselves* proud," Dr. Richards said, giving me an odd look as I smiled at him. He sniffed a couple of times near me, like he was trying to smell my perfume, then toddled off to do the principal thing with all the parents.

"Em, what's wrong with you?" Dru asked, tugging on my arm as Mr. Barlind yelled at us to get into line the way we rehearsed the day before.

"Nothing. I feel faaaaaaaaabuslous."

"Fabuslous? Oh, man, Em, you're stoned!"

"Am not," I said, outraged at her slur. "I haven't smoked anything!"

"Places! Williams, in the rear. Remember—no talking. No funny faces. Your parents and families are watching.

The first person who gets out of line will drop and give me twenty. Everyone got that?"

Dru gave me a worried look, but took her place in the front part of the line. I joined the other Ws, giving them a little wave and cheery smile as I did. The music started over the loudspeakers, and off we marched, Mr. Barlind yelling instructions from behind us.

I didn't get to see where Mom and Brother were sitting because I was too into the whole marching-along-to-the-music thing (I never knew how fun marching could be), but I did bow a couple of times as all the parentals applauded. I thought it was only polite.

Dr. Richards spent a few minutes yakking away, explaining what happened to Caitlin in a way that made me positive he was either Arnold Schwarzenegger in disguise, or an alien. Maybe both.

"Go," the W person next to me said, shoving me half off my chair.

"Hey!" I said, considering walloping him on the head with my cast.

"It's your speech," he said.

"My speech? I'm not the one who sounds like Arnold Schwarzenwhoozits."

"No, it's your turn to do your speech," the W kid (I think his name was Dave, but I couldn't remember for sure, because for some reason my brain seemed to have stopped working).

"Emily Williams!" Dr. Richards bellowed into the microphone, and it was only by the strongest form of self-control that I kept from yelling, "Yo!" back at him. But I remembered in time that this was a big deal, and Brother would probably lecture me for the rest of my life if I messed it up, so I just stood up and gracefully, like a swan on Rollerblades (whoa—bad memory of blading through the streets of Paris—not going there), swayed my way down the aisle to the stage.

I smiled at Dr. Richards to show him I wasn't prejudiced against Schwarzenaliens, then smiled at everyone in the audience, taking a minute to look for Mom and Brother and Bess. I finally found them sitting along one side, Brother with a startled look on his face. I waved at them, and would have blown air kisses, but Dr. Richards made throat-cleary noises, and nudged my hand with the speech in it.

"Oh. Sorry. Forgot," I told him, giggling just a little bit. I giggled even more when the previous giggle, caught by the microphone, filled the gym. People in the audience started laughing then, which made me laugh more, which the microphone picked up, and before you knew it, we were all having a really good time.

"Read. The. Speech," Dr. Richards (who wasn't laughing) hissed at me, his hand over the microphone.

"Sure. That's my job," I told him, then turned to the audience, who had finally stopped laughing. "Hi! I'm Emily. Caitlin was smashed up in a car, but she's OK, and I'm going to read her speech so you guys don't miss it, because I'm sure she spent a long time on it. She's a brainy chick, although kinda snotty to people who don't

83

get into the Mensa stuff like she does, but you know what? To each his own, say I. OK, so, this speech. It says here: 'Welcome Dr. Richards, school board members, Miss Bucwater, faculty, 'rents, fam, and fellow grads'. Only she said *parents* and *family,* but I shortened it because it's so long to say it the right way."

I stopped for a moment to smile at everyone because I thought that opening bit was so nice, and also because I liked smiling. " 'Kay. The rest says: 'We, the graduating class of 2005, have passed a milestone today, and taken a tremendous step forward as we begin the rite of passage into adulthood.' "

I frowned at the page for a minute, the words not making much sense, but I made an effort to read them just as they were written. " 'We are at a turning point in our lives—some of us will go on to college, others will go to trade school, and some will go straight into the workforce. But we will all of us, every member of this great and wonderful family called the class of 2005, continue to learn in order to become a success.' You know, she's absolutely right," I told the audience. "I learned all sorts of things just now standing in the boys' locker room. For one, what's up with urinals? How come they get more places to go to the bathroom than girls get? That's discrimination, and I just hope the school board" I turned to glare at the row where the representatives of the school board were sitting "does something to change that. 'Cause it's just not fair. Anyway, Caitlin is so right about that learning thing. We should learn more stuff, like how to be nicer to each other, and how to set goals and work to get them, not just whine because your best friend got a car for graduation, but your father said you could just drive the family car rather than go to the expense of getting you your own car. Which is lame, but we won't go there. Anyhoodles, Caitlin is right, so you all listen up to her."

I smiled again, pleased by the stunned looks of appreciation on everyone's faces, including the guys in my class. I hummed a little happy song to myself for a couple of seconds, then suddenly remembered that I was supposed to introduce the main speaker.

"Oops, got a little distracted," I said as Dr. Richards lunged for me. "Just a sec, I'm getting to it! Boy, you need to start drinking decaf. 'Kay, listen up, peeps! Today we have an über special guest to talk to everyone. The thing at the bottom of Caitlin's speech says she's won some sort of hair-flipping award. . . ." I squinted at the paper, trying to make the words stop dancing around and stay put so I could read them. "Sorry! Says she won a broadcasting award. Don't know where I got that hair-flipping thing, although . . ." I turned to look at Glenda the weather woman, worried I might have embarrassed her by mentioning the hair thing. You never knew with people, and I figured I'd better give her some props so she wouldn't feel bad. ". . . you do it really, really well. You deserve an award for it."

People started snickering in the audience. I thought about snickering with them, but Dr. Richards was hovering at my side with a really crappy look on his face, so I decided to just get on with it.

"You know," I said, draping myself across the wooden podium that held the microphone. "I've always *liked* aliens—"

"Thank you, Emily Williams," Dr. Richards said, yanking me off the podium and shoving me behind him as he reintroduced Glenda. I thought that was a bit rude, because I had given her a really nice introduction, but I wasn't going to make a stink about it, since it was graduation and all. Mrs. Elliott grabbed me and hauled me off the stage, asking me in a really angry whisper if I had been drinking.

"Just water," I told her as she hustled me down the aisle to where my seat was.

"Then you're high on something."

"Nope. I don't do drugs, 'cause I need my brain to do psychics. Physyms. Chycics. The science thing where you figure out stuff."

"You have embarrassed yourself, the class, and the whole school," she whispered, her hand hurting my arm as she jerked me along. "Dr. Richards will have plenty to say to your parents when the ceremony is over."

"Ow," I protested, wondering why she was being so mean to me. Maybe she and Dr. Richards were in cahoots. "Are you an alien, too?"

She shoved me into my seat and strode off down the aisle without saying another word.

Dave the W kid grinned at me. "Nice speech!"

"She's an alien," I told him. "That proves it."

"Totally."

I kind of dozed the rest of the ceremony, until it was time to march down and get my diploma. I did a couple more bows at the applause, then walked up to Glenda the hair lady to get the diploma.

"Congratulations," she said, giving me kind of an odd glance as she held out the diploma.

"Got an owie," I said, remembering to hold up my cast.

"Er . . ."

I took the diploma, stuffed it under my arm, and held out my left hand to shake hers. She did a little switch of her hands to shake with her left, but as soon as she did the diploma fell out from where it was clamped under my arm (I'd forgotten to put it under my right arm).

"Idiot me," I said, bending down to get it at the same time she did. We clunked heads just as I grabbed it. I reeled backward, rubbing my forehead as she yelped.

Dr. Richards glared at me and ran to see if Glenda was all right. I figured I'd reassure him that I was fine, so it wouldn't stop the ceremony. "Got it!" I said, holding up the diploma, then turned to show it to Mom and Brother. "Yay, me!"

I don't remember a whole lot about the rest of the graduation. I was starting to get really sleepy and pretty much slept through the rest of it. I do remember Dru telling Brother that I'd taken a pain pill.

"She *what?*" Brother yelled, but Mom hushed him

when Dr. Richards came racing over to tattle on me. And tattle he did.

"Dr. Williams, how you can condone the blatantly drunk behavior of Emily—"

"She's not drunk," Brother said, holding up a hand to stop Dr. Richards' tirade. I smiled my very best (A.K.A. Fang) smile at Brother, because even though he had a hair horn, and he lived to give me grief, there were times when he wasn't a bad father. "It's the pain pills she received in Canada for her broken hand. Her mother and I noticed last evening that she seems to have a slight sensitivity where they are concerned, and they tend to make her a bit . . . er . . ."

"Loopy," Bess said, waving at some other kid's sister that she knew. "She only looks drunk, but she's not. Em spews when she drinks, so if she's not barfing, she's not drunk."

"Thank you, Bess, that is very helpful," Brother said, giving her the Eyebrows of Death.

"Regardless of what form of substance abuse she has indulged in, she has ruined the commencement ceremony!" Dr. Richards said in a really mean Klingon voice.

"She hasn't ruined anything," Brother replied, doing his best to be soothing. "And you can hardly call taking drugs prescribed by a doctor substance abuse."

"A foreign doctor," Dr. Richards said suspiciously.

"He was sooooo hot, too," I said, doing my part to

calm everyone down. I had a brilliant thought at that moment.

"But still a qualified physician who knew exactly what he was doing," Brother pointed out.

"I shall now do an interpretive dance that explores the exact hottie nature of the hunkalicious Dr. Grant," I announced, and proceeded to do a happy little dance that I figured would do a lot to get everyone to stop yelling and start singing again.

"There, you see? She is clearly under the influence of foreign drugs, drugs not tested by the FDA. This is exactly the sort of thing we can expect from foreign influences!"

Brother looked at him like he had an entire toolbox of screws loose. "We're talking about Canada, correct?"

"I will write to my congressman," Dr. Richards said, a militant light making his eyes shine just like an alien monster's right before it chomps on Sigourney Weaver. "I will not allow this abuse to go unprotested!"

He walked away making notes in a tiny black notebook.

"That man is loopier than Emily," Brother said to Mom, who had been standing behind him with one hand over her mouth like she was A) going to barf or B) trying not to laugh. I did a spur-of-the-moment dance in honor of barf, but stopped when she laughed.

"Come along, Martha Graham, let's get you home before you cause any more trouble," Mom said, pushing me down the aisle through all the other people hanging around, yakking and singing and I swear, some of them were turning into sunflowers.

That's really all I remember until I woke up the following morning.

So see? None of it was my fault. Stuff like that always happens to me. I'm going to go call the Wiccan chick and see if she knows any de-cursing spells.

Hope you are feeling better. What did the doctor say when you saw him this morning? Did you tell him we're going on a cruise in less than three weeks? A romantic cruise, just the two of us (and a boatload of other people, but we don't know them).

Massive hugs and oodles of kisses,
Emily

Subject: Re: It's hopeless
From: Emster@seattlegrrl.com
To: Hollyberry@britsahoy.co.uk
Date: June 23, 2005 2:02 pm

> *everything is all buggered up. I honestly want to cry,*
> *Em. I was so looking forward to seeing you this sum-*
> *mer, but Mum says now that she can't trust me to*
> *travel alone because Pearson and I went to London*
> *while she was in the Lake District, but you know that*
> *nothing happened! We stayed in a youth hostel! It's*
> *so unfair!*

That totally is, and I don't blame you one bit for being so pissy with your mom. I mean, you're seventeen! You're not an infant! However, take it from someone who has had eons of practical experience with parents so old they make Stonehenge look like something out of a cheap music video—sometimes you just have to admit you were wrong, and give the song and dance about never, ever doing it again, and how you've learned your lesson, yadda, yadda, shoot me now so I don't have to say it over and over and over again.

Anyhoo, sometimes you just have to get that out of the way so you can then move on to the negotiating stage, where you get what you want by pointing out that you've learned from your mistakes, and need to have new experiences to grow and all that crap.

> *Pearson is . . . meh. He's not a BF. He's just a guy. But*
> *he's nice and he's going to uni and I like him, just not*
> *that way, you know? That's the other thing that*
> *makes me want to cry a lot. Ever since I broke up with*
> *Ruaraidh last year, I haven't had a boyfriend last*
> *longer than a month. Something's wrong with me, I*
> *just know it! I'm a pariah!*

OK, I had to go look *pariah* up. I thought for a mo you meant Mariah and just mistyped it, and I wondered if you were going with a new name, because I think Mariah is cool, but there were two Mariahs already in our class back in Piddlington, so it would be kind of lame to make yourself Mariah III. Unless you really like the name, and then who cares? But I see that *pariah* means, like, a social leper, so OK. Gotcha on that.

And you are so not a social leper! You have tons of friends! You're Miss Outgoing now! So you don't have a snog partner at the moment. So what? Yeah, it's kinda bad, but you know I went for *months* waiting for Fang, and then almost a month after he came back with the Evil One (who, OK, turned out to be not so evil), so I know what I'm talking about. You don't need a BF. They're nice to have around, but I'm living proof that you can actually survive without one. You're sweet, and you're interesting, and darn it, people *like* you!

Hee. Sorry. Was watching a *Saturday Night Live* DVD. That guy who does the Stuart Smalley thingie is pretty funny.

Hey, do you hear anything from Ruaraidh anymore? I wonder how his eleventh finger is doing.

> *you going to the college to see your dorm next*
> *week? Are your parents going too, or will it be just*
> *you and Dru? Say hi to Fang for me, and give him a*
> *hug. I sure miss talking to him, although he did*
> *e-mail me a couple of days ago to tell me thank you*
> *for the birthday card I sent him a while ago.*

happy sigh He is *so* the perfect Mr. Emily. Or he would be if he'd just *get well.* I'm going up this weekend to see the college and do the tour thing with the parentals, so I won't have any quality Fang time in which to practice my new kissing technique. Which is a shame, because I finally have come up with what I think is the definitive description of what goes into the perfect kiss. Dru won't be coming with us because she's decided to go to the Ewe Dub (a.k.a. University of Washington) so she can live at home and save money for the gazillion-dollar wedding she's determined to have.

No wedding talk. I refuse to do wedding talk.

Hugsters! Lots of them!
~Em

You have a Chat Girl Instant Message. Click to receive it.

GonnaMarryFelix: Whatcha doing?
Em=c^2: Just got done e-mailing Holly. She thinks she's a pariah.
GonnaMarryFelix: Huh?
Em=c^2: Pariah. Go look it up.
GonnaMarryFelix: Man, you and your Word a Day thing.
Em=c^2: This isn't mine; it's Holly's. I had to look it up, too.
GonnaMarryFelix: Oh.
GonnaMarryFelix: Looking.

GonnaMarryFelix: OK, so she thinks she's this pariah. Why does she think that?

Em=c^2: She is currently –BF.

GonnaMarryFelix: Ouch.

Em=c^2: Yeah.

GonnaMarryFelix: Did you tell her she doesn't need one? Did you tell her about empowering the goddess within, and that no woman needs a man to complete her?

Em=c^2: I did my Stuart Smalley impression for her. Only it didn't work too well in e-mail. Oooh! Hold on, Fang on the phone.

GonnaMarryFelix: OK.

GonnaMarryFelix: Say hi for me.

Em=c^2: He says hi back, and told me to tell you that the next time we're in B.C. and I break my hand, would you please call him and let him know we need help?

GonnaMarryFelix: Heh.

GonnaMarryFelix: Em?

GonnaMarryFelix: You still there?

GonnaMarryFelix: You're not having phone sex with him, are you?

Em=c^2: Ew! No! He's telling me about what the doctor he saw the other day said.

GonnaMarryFelix: What's wrong with him?

Em=c^2: Not sure. The doctor thought at first it might be mumps, which has Fang all weirded out.

GonnaMarryFelix: Mumps? Why?

Em=c^2: Asking.

Em=c^2: Erm . . .

GonnaMarryFelix: What?

Em=c^2: Evidently if you're a guy and you're an adult and you get mumps, it can mean you can't have kids.

GonnaMarryFelix: *What?*

Em=c^2: Yeah, he says it does something to their . . . you know . . . sperm and stuff.

GonnaMarryFelix: Ew! TMI!

Em=c^2: Tell me about it. He's going into details on just what the mumps does.

Em=c^2: Bleargh.

GonnaMarryFelix: That bad?

Em=c^2: Remind me never to have a medical discussion with an almost-vet while I'm trying to eat lunch.

GonnaMarryFelix: Yuck.

Em=c^2: Oh, it's OK. The doctor finally decided today that it wasn't mumps. Whew.

GonnaMarryFelix: That's good. I mean, if you guys get married, you'll want to have kids and all.

Em=c^2: Phhht.

GonnaMarryFelix: So what does he have?

Em=c^2: Don't know. He's still getting to it. He keeps telling me it'll be all right, and not to worry about anything.

GonnaMarryFelix: Which, of course, makes you really worried.

Em=c^2: Oh, yeah.

Em=c^2: OK, I think it's coming now.

Em=c^2: He's just said that it's not going to stop him

from going on the cruise, so whatever it is, it can't be too serious.

Em=c^2: Oh.

Em=c^2: My.

Em=c^2: *God!!!!!!!!!*

GonnaMarryFelix: What? *What????*

Em=c^2: I have to go. I have to go look up *mono* online.

GonnaMarryFelix: Mono? Omigod! He doesn't!

Em=c^2: My life is over.

GonnaMarryFelix: OMG!!!!!

Em=c^2: *sniffle*

GonnaMarryFelix: Well . . . that's curable, right? Didn't your sister have it for a while?

Em=c^2: Yeah, when we were in sixth grade. But this is different! Bess was in middle school then, and Fang and I are adults!

GonnaMarryFelix: Ouch. That means . . .

Em=c^2: Wah! I have a romantic cruise coming up with the dishiest BF in the whole, wide world, a guy who makes me dance and sing whenever I see him, a guy so numalicious I practically drool whenever I'm near him, and I can't even kiss him!

GonnaMarryFelix: Man, Em. Sometimes, your life really sucks.

Em=c^2: Waaaaaaaaaaaaaaaaaaaaah!

Subject: Sigh
From: Emster@seattlegrrl.com
To: Fbaxter@doormouse.ca
Date: June 23, 2005 8:23 pm

> *It's not really that bad. I'm on antibiotics, and my*
> *throat is already feeling better. I'm worried about*
> *you, though. You're sure you're not feeling the least*
> *bit sick? The incubation period for mono is anywhere*
> *between a month and two months, and since I came*
> *down to see you for your birthday party two months*
> *ago . . . I worry, love.*

Melty, melty, melt, melt over the *love*. I love it when you love me! Love, love, love!

OK, floating back to earth. Mom just walked by my bedroom and gave me a really weird look because I was singing that John Lennon love song. No need to worry, Fangypants, I'm fine, other than having a broken hand and a snogalicious boyfriend I can't kiss for . . . what, forever? I know it's only for a few months, but it's going to seem like forever. Especially with the cruise . . . Sigh.

OK, I'm not going to do the Saint Emily the Martyr thing here. I'm an adult. I am thinking about you, not me, and what's best for you is to have lots and lots of rest, and not to worry, and to drink lots of soup. And if you aren't feeling well enough to go on the cruise . . . well, we'll just miss it, that's all.

insert broken-hearted music here

> *didn't tell you on the phone because Kevin was in the*
> *room, and he's even sicker than I am. We figured out*
> *that the mono came from his girlfriend, Claudia. She*
> *was here last month, and . . . There's no way to tell this*
> *but just to say it. She got drunk one night and tried to*
> *snog me. You know me well enough to know I don't*
> *go around kissing other women, Emily, so you can stop*
> *making that "Fang doesn't love me! Fang is kissing*
> *other women!" face that I'm certain you're making.*
> *You're the only one for me, love, and you know it.*

I am not making a face. I'm not making any face. I'm sitting here perfectly calm and collected and not in the least bit wanting to scream or yell *or go up to Canada to* BEAT THE CRAP OUT OF THIS CLAUDIA PERSON *BECAUSE SHE TRIED TO STEAL MY BOYFRIEND!*

No, I am perfectly sane.

Aaaaaaaaaaaaaaaaarrrrrrrrrrrgh!

OK, now I'm perfectly sane. Just had to get that little scream out. I trust you, Fang. I really do. I'm not going to make a big deal about this. I can totally understand anyone wanting to kiss you.

But that doesn't mean I'm ever going to forgive her for ruining our wonderful formerly romantic, now-just-scenic cruise! And for making you suffer, of course.

> *The cruise should be just fine, so long as you don't*
> *mind me being a bit spotty. I've got a bit of a rash (I*

> *look like I've got the measles), but the doctor says it*
> *should clear up soon. He did tell me to limit any*
> *strenuous activities, so I'm going to have to cut back*
> *on my rounds with Dr. Wu. Worst time for that, too,*
> *since we are right in the middle of cattle vaccinations,*
> *but the doc says the pain in my side is because my*
> *spleen is enlarged. I've got some antibiotics for the*
> *staph throat, too, so you don't have to worry about*
> *that.*

Oh, my God. Omigod! Your spleen is erupting? I read about that on the Mono 'n' You page! They say that can kill you! Eeeeeeeeeeek! Don't do anything! Just sit around and get better. OMG! Should I come up and take care of you? I should, shouldn't I? A good girlfriend would go up and take care of her poor, sick, exploding-spleen BF. We're all going up to Carlyle this weekend, but maybe I should stay there for a while and make you sit and rest and let your spleen de—whatever it is that it's doing?

I'm back. I had to get a cup of tea. While I was there, Bess came in and . . . Sigh.

"How can you tell if you're cursed?" I asked Bess while she was swiping some of Mom's Earl Grey tea. (I like the local Market Spice tea better—it's really orangey and spicy and . . . oh, yeah, I made you try it the last time you were here, didn't I? Was that the tea you called Chick Tea?)

"What are you on about now?" Bess asked, using her

English accent on me (her BF, Monk—you remember him? The guy from the south of England who was going to become a Buddhist monk, but got into the dot-com business instead?—was here a couple of weeks ago, so she's been überly English-ified ever since).

"I think I'm cursed. It's like everything in my life is going to hell."

"Karma," Bess said, hunting for some cookies to go with the tea.

"Oh, no, don't you start that too! I've had it up to here with karma," I said, doing exasperated hand gestures. "Karma can just go stick itself where the sun don't shine. I'm serious, Bess. My life is ruined! I have broken fingers, half the people in my school—former school, now that I don't go there anymore—think I'm a drug fiend, the other half is trying to hit me up for pain pills, and now this!"

"Now what?" she asked, nuking a mug of water.

"Fang!" I said, waving my hands around in the air. My cast clunked into the frig and knocked off a ceramic nudie that Mom had painted when she was transitioning from ceramics to canvas painting. It hit the floor and smashed into a billion pieces. "Oh, great, now I broke Mom's naked refrigerator woman!"

"See? I told you. Karma. What else is going wrong besides you destroying Mom's art?"

I shot Bess a nasty look as I scooped up the bits of the broken woman. "If karma is going to get anyone in this family, it's going to be an older sister who doesn't have any sort of sympathy at all. Fang is what's wrong."

"What's up with the Fang man?" she asked, stirring a couple of spoonfuls of sugar into her tea before taking a sip. "He dump you for some brawny Canadian farmer girl?"

"Oh, you're sooo funny I laughed up my . . . spleen!"

"Em?" Bess set down her cup of tea when I slid down the refrigerator to the floor and burst into tears. "What's going on? Fang hasn't really dumped you, has he? He's head-over-heels in love with you."

"It's not that," I said, wiping at my face with the dish towel, which is kind of gross, but there was nothing else to use, and I didn't want my nose running all over the place. "Fang is sick. He's wounded! He could die!"

"Ouch," she said, frowning when I told her about the mono. "That's bad. It was horrible when I had it, but I can imagine it's much worse in an adult. How's he feeling?"

"He says better. But his spleen is about to blow up, and I won't be able to kiss him or anything on our cruise, and everything in my life sucks so much I just have to be cursed!"

"Sounds to me like you're going through a rough period is all, but I'll ask Silver."

"Silver the Wiccan person who heads up your meadow?"

"It's a grove, not a meadow." Bess grabbed a box of

Kleenex and brought it over to me. "And yes, that Silver. She knows something about the black arts, so if you're cursed, she should be able to tell us what to do. But seriously Em, I just think this is a crappy time for you."

I'm not so sure, Fang. I mean, bad stuff has happened to me before, but not anything where *you could die!*

And all because of that Claudia . . . um. What was her last name again? I know you told me, but I don't remember.

Go lie down and sleep. Sleep is really good for you when you're sick. Mom always says that when you're sick, sleep makes you better faster because you recharge your batteries. So go sleep and don't get up except to eat and e-mail me. And go to the bathroom, of course, because otherwise—ick!

Big, big hugs. No kisses, though. Which makes me want to cry. Sigh.
Emily (worried!)

Subject: Hmm.
From: Emster@seattlegrrl.com
To: Hollyberry@britsahoy.co.uk
Date: June 24, 2005 10:11 am

We're just getting ready to leave for Canada, but I wanted to tell you that Bess's Wiccan friend says I'm not cursed.

I think she's fibbing, though. Her face turned all red

when she read my tea leaves, and she hurried out of the house before Mom could stuff her with breakfast.

Suspicious, huh?

Hope you're resting and stuff. We should be there in about five hours, assuming Brother doesn't get us arrested going across the border. You just never know with him. Anyhoo, massive, massive hugs and kisses and those little tickles around your ears that you said make you shiver.

Love you!
Emily

Subject: Re: Erm . . .
From: Emster@seattlegrrl.com
To: Hollyberry@britsahoy.co.uk
Date: June 26, 2005 11:40 pm

> *Um, Em? Did you mean that e-mail to go to me? Or*
> *was it for Fang? Why did you*

Sorry! Sorry, sorry, sorry! I was going to reply to your message, but then Brother started having a meltdown about how long it would take to drive to Canada, so I meant to send Fang a quick note.

> *think you were cursed? How did the college visit go?*
> *Did you stay an extra day like you wanted to? How's*
> *Fang?*

Look at my life, Holly. Just look at it! If I'm not cursed, who is? Anyway, as you saw, Bess's Wiccan leader woman said I wasn't cursed; I just have crappy luck. But I'm going to get a second opinion. Dru knows of a Cajun woman in Pioneer Square (it's an old part of Seattle full of street people, pigeons, and lots of *touristas*) who does clairvoyance and things, so we're going to go to her this week and see if I've got an evil eye or something on me.

College visit . . . ooooh. It's the one good thing in all the bad. No, wait, Fang is the one good thing in all the bad, but right now he's part of the bad, and he can't be on the good and bad sides at the same time, can he? So that makes college the one good thing.

Despite the embarrassment of having to go with the units *de* parentals, it was pretty cool.

"It's small," Brother said as we walked across the visitor parking area to the big administration building that sat on one corner of the campus. "It has to be a tenth of the size of the UW. I bet their enrollment isn't even five thousand."

"Small isn't necessarily bad," Mom said as she pulled out the letter I'd given her inviting me to visit the campus as a prospective international student.

"Ah, that must be their library," Brother said, veering off to the side.

Mom grabbed his arm to keep him from leaving. "We'll be late for the appointment with the dean of students if we stop to see their library."

"Bah." Brother looked grouchy, but he let Mom tug

him along to the big brick admin building. There weren't a lot of people on the campus because it was a Saturday, and only summer classes were going on, but I did see a bunch of people lying out on a grassy square lined with big buildings (I found out later it's called the quad, for *quadrangle*). "Probably don't have much of interest anyway."

"It is a university that emphasizes technical rather than esoteric study," Mom pointed out as we followed the signs to the dean's office.

"They have a good physics program," I added.

"Esoteric?" Brother said, still grumpy. "Since when are early medieval Britain studies considered esoteric?"

Mom and I gave him looks. He grumbled. I walked behind the old ones, looking around at everything even though I knew I was going to go to this college (it had Fang! No other college could come even close to matching that), although Mom insisted that we visit the college before they agreed to shell out the bucks for it.

"It's small, it probably has no one teaching courses in Low and Middle English, and yet I'm expected to entrust them with the education of my youngest child?" Brother asked no one in particular.

I rolled my eyes and slowed down, so it didn't look like I was with them. Mom thwapped Brother on the arm. "It also takes combined SAT scores of eleven hundred for admission, the teacher to student ratio is lower than UW's, and the cost of sending Emily to school here is a third of what it would be back home."

That shut Brother up for a while. He may be an academic snob sometimes, but he also liked the fact that I could go to school here, live in a dorm, and get a new laptop (included in the tuition) for a ton less money than it would cost for me to go to another school.

We did the chat-with-the-dean stuff, during which Mom asked all sorts of practical questions. Brother sniffed a lot, but looked interested when the dean (old guy, no chin, ears that waggled when he talked) said he had a history degree, and was interested in ye olde medieval stuff (he didn't say it that way, though). I looked out the window and wondered how Fang was doing. The whole thing of checking out the school was pointless, as far as I was concerned—you know I made my mind up to go here as soon as Fang transferred from that college in England.

Since I'd already received an acceptance to Carlyle, I didn't do an interview or anything, but we did get coupons for free food at one of the cafs.

"And I understand that Emily wishes to sit in on classes?" the dean, named Dr. Sayer, asked, shuffling through some papers to find one with my name on it.

"Yeah, that would be really cool," I said, trying to look like I wasn't sure I wanted to go here, even though I really did. Mom had said I could take the train back to Seattle on Monday if I wanted to do the visiting-student thing, and who am I to turn down an extra day with Fang?

"Excellent. Here is the name and location of your host student. She'll be expecting you after dinner. If you have any questions, don't hesitate to ask her or any of the other students. I'm sure you'll find that everyone at Carlyle is very friendly, and supportive of our American cousins."

Gacky, huh? I thought so, too. Anyhoodles, Mom did the mom-chat thing with the dean a bit more; then we toddled off to see the library (Brother insisted). But as soon as we got to the door of the admin building, I screamed and flung myself down the steps to the cobblestone courtyard area outside it.

"Fang!"

"Oh, Lord," Brother muttered behind me as I ran to the man just at the bottom of the steps. "Look, Chris, it's the boyfriend."

"Fang, Fang, Fang," I yelled as I leaped down the stairs and threw myself on him.

Fang is smart. I think we both agree on that, right? But this is just how smart he is—rather than fall over backward and crack his head like Devon, Fang saw me coming and took a protective stance with the big metal handrail behind him to brace him. So when I jumped him, wrapping my arms and legs around him, he didn't topple like . . . well, like something big with something else big on it, falling over (man, I'll never forget knocking him down in that airport). Nope, not my BF. He just said "Emily!" and hugged me as I kissed him all over his face (except his lips, which was a shame because he's got the most nummy lips, but I won't go into details because it'll just make me cry).

"Oh!" I said, stopping the face kissing for a mo. "It's OK if I kiss your cheeks, right? I won't get mono from your skin, will I?"

"No, it's fine if you kiss me there," he said, smiling at me, his lurvley brown eyes all twinkly and happy at me. "So long as you don't mind the rash."

He did look like he had a light case of measles, but I wasn't going to let that stop me. I kissed him everywhere I could, hugged him even tighter, and told him how happy I was to see him.

"Francis," Brother said, nodding at Fang when I finally peeled myself off him.

"Henry," Fang said, nodding back, which made me smile. Brother hates to be called by his real name almost as much as Fang hates to be called by his. It's a little thing they do. I think it's kind of cute, but it drives Brother nuts when Fang calls him Henry. Hee.

They did the guy handshake thingie; then Fang gave me a bouquet of flowers he had been holding, which made me squee like mad, which meant, of course, that I had to kiss him some more because it'd been months since I'd seen him.

"Would you like to see the campus?" Fang asked after I was through with the whole kissing thing, and Mom had exchanged polite chitchat with Fang like she always does with my friends. "I can show you around a bit, if you'd like."

"Eek!" I said. "Your spleen! Stop walking! Sit down! Where is it? Is it bulging out or something?"

"Dear God, Chris, she's groping him right here in front of us! She gets that from your side of the family. My side never gropes," Brother said as I patted Fang's sides for his spleen, wondering just what I was going to do if I could feel it all swollen and explodey and stuff.

"For which you should be glad of my hearty peasant stock bringing life to your blue blood," Mom said calmly. "Groping is much more fun than being able to trace your family tree back to a bunch of dusty English kings."

"Emily." Fang laughed, grabbing my hands. "My spleen isn't on my waist, and it's not bulging. I can walk around, just nothing strenuous."

"Oh," I said, giving Brother a quick glare when he made another snarky crack. "Excuse me, Fang could die if his spleen erupts! That gives me, his very concerned girlfriend, the right to conduct spleen checks. Um." I looked back at Fang, who was wiping tears from his eyes. "Where exactly is your spleen?"

"Right here," he said, putting my hand on his chest, where his heart was.

"That's your heart."

"My spleen is also in there. It's protected by my rib cage, so you don't have to worry about it bursting out of my body," he said, still laughing.

"OK." I gave his chest a pat. "You just keep it happy in there, all right?"

He stopped walking to hug me, kissing my ear and whispering, "Ah, Em. You're so good for me. I've missed you."

I went all melty at that, of course, because who wouldn't? Brother rolled his eyes a lot, but I totally ignored him while Fang showed us around the campus.

"The physics compound is over there, I think," he said, pointing vaguely toward a couple of buildings. "And ahead is one of the vet buildings."

"Oooh," I said, looking at a big brick structure. Not much to it, but just the thought of Fang hanging out there made it cool. "What classes are you taking now?"

"This semester is light because of the fieldwork I'm doing with Dr. Wu, but I'm taking clinical virology, ruminant surgery and medicine, and swine health monitoring."

"Wow," I said, totally impressed even though it was just Fang. He looked so serious when he talked vet stuff, it always gave me goose bumps. "Sounds really cool. Clinical virology!"

"It must be the real thing," Brother muttered to Mom. "Only true love could find ruminant medicine fascinating."

"I so defather you," I said, pointing a finger at Brother.

"What?" he said, his eyes wide, like he was all surprised.

"You're making fun of Fang and me!"

"No, I'm making fun of the fact that you're so enamored with him that you'd find swine health monitoring a subject of great interest," Brother answered. He had that annoying look on his face. (You know—the one that makes him look like he's just eaten half a cheesecake and isn't telling anyone where he's hidden the other half.) The fact that he could joke about something so serious as Fang potentially dying just made me furious. So that's my excuse for what followed.

"Well, I am just sorry that you don't have someone who loves you and gives a damn about what you do!" I said, stopping and glaring at Brother. "But I do care about what Fang does!"

"Now you're being hypocritical," Brother said, glaring right back at me. "You won't even eat pork but you find swine medicine thrilling?"

"Emily, it doesn't matter—" Fang started to say.

"Yes, it does!" I told him. "He's making fun of us because I'm interested in things you are doing. He knows that Mom doesn't like medieval stuff, so he's lashing out. He's *mocking* us!"

"No, he's not." Fang started laughing again. I clapped a hand over his chest.

"Stop laughing! I bet that's making your spleen move around and stuff!"

"Your mother loves medieval history," Brother said, looking offended. "Chris, tell the spawn that you love medieval history."

Fang laughed even harder.

Mom said nothing.

"Chris?"

"Well . . ." Mom did a little hand gesture that pretty much said, *I hate medieval stuff*.

"Chris!" Brother said, looking mean at her.

Fang laughed so hard tears leaked out the corners of his eyes.

"See what you've done?" I said, waving one hand at Brother while holding back Fang's spleen with the other. "You're probably going to cause him to explode and die, and then I'll die too, of a broken heart! I just hope you'll be happy then, Mr. Ha Ha!"

"The only thing he's likely to die of here is you shoving your hand through his pectoral muscle," Brother said, rolling his eyes yet again.

"Gah!" I yelled.

"Brother, stop picking on Emily," Mom said, giving him a warning look.

"Yeah," I said. "See? Even Mom is siding with me."

"And Emily, you can stop baiting your father."

"I am *so* not baiting—"

Mom gave me one of those Mom looks. I decided it wasn't dignified of me to fight in front of Fang. Besides, I wanted him to stop laughing and rest, so I just smiled at him; gave his spleen area a couple of "think happy, unexploding thoughts" pats, and spent the next hour ignoring Brother as much as I could.

By the time we walked (slowly, 'cause of Fang) around the campus, it was close to dinnertime. Mom wanted us to find a restaurant and have a nice dinner out, but Brother, as usual, was being obstinate.

"We have food vouchers," he said, waving the bits of paper that the dean guy had given him.

"I think it would be much nicer to have dinner in a

restaurant," Mom said. "This is a college town—there must be any number of good places to eat nearby. Fang, what would you recommend?"

Fang looked thoughtful. "Well . . ."

"It's going to cost me enough to send Emily to college," Brother said in a loud voice. "Now you want me to spend even more on meals out?"

"Dear, it's not that much."

"Every penny counts," Brother argued, his face getting all red like it does when he's annoyed.

"That's it! You're no longer my father," I said, holding on to Fang's hand (that was another squee moment, but I won't go into how really romantic it was to walk around holding his hand). "I formally disown you as my parent. Buh-bye."

"If I am no longer your father, then I don't have to pay your tuition," he said, giving me a squinty-eyed look.

"I'm refathering you," I said after a couple of seconds' thought. "But you're on probation!"

Fang snorted, but didn't outright laugh, which was good, because I think his spleen had probably just about had enough.

We ended up giving in to Brother's little temper tantrum (he's such a drama queen! Thank God I don't take after that side of the fam) and ate at one of the college cafeterias. I actually didn't care where we ate, so long as it was close by and Fang would sit and rest, and I could sit next to him and look at him whenever I wanted to, and play footsies, and kneesies, and a cou-

ple of times I smiled a special smile at him. You know—
the one that says that if he didn't have mono, and we
were alone together on a cruise ship, staying in the
same cabin, *things* might happen. *Important* things.

After a long lecture about not breaking anything, not
spending any money, and general "behave yourself"
crap, Mom and Brother finally left so they'd get home
before it was dark.

I stood with Fang in the parking lot, watching them
leave.

"Man," I said to Fang once the car was out of sight.
"I don't know what's wrong with Brother lately, but I'm
really sorry he was such a pain tonight."

Fang wrapped an arm around me and pulled me
close like he was going to kiss me. Only he couldn't, of
course. He just smiled at me instead, his brown eyes all
happy and smiley too. "Don't you know?"

"Know what? Are you sure I can't kiss you just a little
bit? One without, you know, tonguey action?"

He laughed and kissed the tip of my nose. (Nose
melty time! Ew. Wait. That sounds gross. Never mind.)
"I don't think I could stand to kiss you without getting
my tongue involved, Em, and I'd never forgive myself if I
infected you. So we'll just keep things mouth-free for a
couple of months, all right?"

I sighed.

He hugged me again. "Have I told you lately how
much you mean to me?"

"No, and I'd punish you for that, but you've been sick, and I don't want Mr. Spleen to get mad at me. So you're off the hook until you're better."

"Then I'd better make the most of such generosity," he said. I smacked him with my flowers (but not hard, because I didn't want to hurt them).

We sat and talked for a couple of hours. I won't bore you with what we talked about, not that Fang's boring, but you know how it is with a BF—a lot of stuff you talk about sounds silly when you tell someone else. So we just sat under a tree and watched people play soccer and toss Frisbees for dogs, and lie around catching the last bit of sun.

"I suppose I should get you to where you're supposed to be going," Fang said once the shadows from a nearby tree crept across us and made me shiver. He stood up and held out his hand to pull me up (squee moment number thirty-four). I ignored it, because I didn't want to strain his innards, but I took it once I was up. "Which dorm is it?"

"Um . . . says McClendon Residence Hall," I said, pulling out the info sheet the dean had handed to me. "The girl I'm staying with is Jessi Benton. Do you know her?"

"No, but I don't know too many people outside the vet program."

"You know," I said, very sneaky and all, "I could always stay with *you* instead."

He shot me a look, but I saw the corners of his mouth curl up like he was trying not to smile. "With a sick roommate and nowhere to sleep but with me?"

I batted my lashes at him.

"You're incorrigible, love," he said, giving me a quick kiss (on the cheek, poop). "There's no way I could stand that temptation. I am human, you know."

"Oh, yes," I said, waggling my eyebrows. "I know."

"Emily," he said, giving me a pretend stern look. "Didn't I hear your father forbid you to seduce me?"

I squeezed his hand as we started off toward a dorm-looking building (ugly, lots of tiny windows). "Yeah, but he says that whenever I go anywhere. If I go to the mall, it's, 'Emily, do not seduce the Orange Julius attendant.' If I go to the movies, it's, 'No sex with the ticket boy.' But the best is the time Dru and I went to her aunt's wedding, and he forbade me to hook up with the choirboys."

He laughed again, but a little laugh, so it was OK. I was a bit disappointed he didn't want me to stay with him, but I had to admit that with his roomie all sick, it probably wasn't the best of ideas. So we toddled to the dorm where I'd spend the night, and asked around until we found my "host student."

"Hi, I'm Emily," I said, holding out my hand.

Jessi, who was taller than me, but had really thin, limp blond hair, smiled a perky little smile and shook my hand before eyeing Fang.

"This is Fang. He's English. He's in the vet program here. And he's *mine*," I said, just so she had that last bit really clear in her mind.

Fang smiled.

"Oh. OK. Hi, I'm Jessi, that's Jessi with no E. Welcome to Carlyle! If you have questions, just fire away."

"Thanks," I said. "It looks like a good school."

"I'm going to leave you now, love," Fang said, giving my fingers a little squeeze.

"Are you all worn out?" I asked, worried about all the walking we'd done. "Maybe you should take a taxi home or something."

"No, it's just a few blocks. I'll be all right. Stop worrying about me."

Poop. Dru's having a hissy about something in IM. Be right back.

Emmers

You have a Chat Girl Instant Message. Click to receive it.

GonnaMarryFelix: Em!
GonnaMarryFelix: Em, what are you doing?
GonnaMarryFelix: EMILY!!!!!!!
Em=c^2: Fwah! I'm right here! I'm telling Holly about my weekend at college, and you just interrupted my flow. Now it'll be all disjointed and stuff. What is so im-

portant that you had to use seven exclamation points and yell at me?

GonnaMarryFelix: Omigod, I just got an e-mail from Felix!

Em=c^2: /me sighs.

Em=c^2: That's all?

GonnaMarryFelix: No!!!

Em=c^2: Well, then, what's boppin'?

GonnaMarryFelix: OMG!

Em=c^2: *yawns*

Em=c^2: It's late, chicky. I want to finish up that e-mail to Holly; then I have to send Fang some stuff about our cruise, and then I have to pick classes really quickly before fall enrollment ends.

GonnaMarryFelix: Fine! I'll tell you! But you'll be sorry you were so unfeeling when you hear the horrible, soul-destroying event that happened to Felix!

Em=c^2: Soul-destroying, huh? What, did he get kicked out of church or something?

GonnaMarryFelix: *Emily!*

Em=c^2: Stop yelling and just spit it out.

GonnaMarryFelix: Felix has been *shot!*

Em=c^2: Shot? OMG!

GonnaMarryFelix: You see? Soul-destroying!

Em=c^2: Well . . . I don't think you can actually shoot a soul. Is he OK? Where did he get shot?

GonnaMarryFelix: His earlobe!

Em=c^2: His ear? He got shot in the ear? Did it go into his brain?

GonnaMarryFelix: No, not his ear—his earlobe! It was shot *completely off!*

Em=c^2: Ouchie. Who shot his earlobe off?

GonnaMarryFelix: Well . . . he did. It was an accident. His gun fired without him knowing it, and it shot his earlobe off.

Em=c^2: /me giggles.

GonnaMarryFelix: Em! It's not funny! He's been *mutilated!*

Em=c^2: Well, I know it must hurt and stuff, but you have to admit, shooting your own earlobe off is kinda funny.

GonnaMarryFelix: It is not! He could have killed himself!

GonnaMarryFelix: Em?

GonnaMarryFelix: You're laughing right now, aren't you?

Em=c^2: Sorry. Tears streaming down face. Can't stop laughing.

GonnaMarryFelix: Gah!

GonnaMarryFelix: I didn't laugh when you told me about Fang's blown-up bladder!

Em=c^2: Spleen, not bladder, and that's totally different. Fang really could die from that, and I think the worst thing that could happen to Felix is that he won't be able to wear an earring on that ear.

GonnaMarryFelix: I am *so* not talking to you right now. You're just inhuman!

Chat Girl GonnaMarryFelix has left.

Subject: Re: Then what?
From: Emster@seattlegrrl.com
To: Hollyberry@britsahoy.co.uk
Date: June 27, 2005 12:33 pm

> *Em! You can't just leave me hanging like that! What*
> *was Dru having a hissy about? And how were the*
> *classes you sat in on? What did you think of the*
> *dorm?*

Gah. Major sorries, Hol. Mom came in right as I was going to finish up, and demanded to know why I was laughing so loudly at almost midnight. So then I had to tell her about Felix shooting his earlobe off (that's what Dru's hissy was about), and then she wanted to see the catalog for the college and stuff, and then I got tired. But I'm here now, so I'll fill you in on the rest of the stuff.

I just registered online, BTW. Fall quarter is going to be dullsville because even though I did some AP stuff in high school, I still have to get some core-curriculum crap out of the way. I mean, sheesh, I don't need rounding out. I don't know why they assume I do. But whatever.

So, back to the weekend. Fang toddled off to his dorm, leaving me with Jessi Without An E (henceforth refered to as JWAE). "Well, this is the lobby and common room, as you can see," JWAE said, waving her hand around at a small room with a bunch of tables and no one in it. "It's a little empty right now, but it can get very full on hockey nights. My room is on the third floor. Elevator is this way. Er . . . did you bring a bag or anything?"

I patted my backpack. "I travel light."

"Oh, OK. Well, onward!"

She yammered about the dorm as we went up to the third floor. "We have a resident director who handles big stuff like thefts and things, and each floor has a resident assistant. Our floor RA does squat, but that's OK—everyone here is pretty nice and we haven't had any problem. Smilies."

I blinked at her a couple of times. "Huh?"

She stopped in front of one of the doors in a long white hallway. "I said our RA is bit of a prat, but he's OK."

"No, you said something about smiles?"

She smiled a happy, perky smile that made me think of psycho killers on Prozac. "Oh, that! Smilies! You know, colon right paren?"

Honest to Pete, Holly, I just stared at her for a couple of seconds. "You mean a computer smiley?"

"You got it. And here's home away from home."

She opened up the door and waved me into the room. I went in slowly. "So . . . instead of just smiling, you actually said—"

"Smilies!" she said, making air quotes.

I didn't say anything, Hol. I wanted to, but I didn't say anything. Diplomacy and all that crap. (Besides, I had to sleep in the same room as her, and I didn't want to cheese her off so she did something weird like spit in my ear while I was sleeping.) Instead I just looked around the dorm room, and sat on the bed she said I could use (her roommate isn't taking classes during the summer). It was a pretty normal dorm room, except on JWAE's wall there were hundreds of cut out butterflies.

"That's really . . . pretty," I said, trying to count them.

"Thank you! I heart my butterflies. They make me feel so happy whenever I'm down!"

Yeah. She said "heart." I'm sayin', is all.

"So tell me all about Fang! He's English? How did you meet him? How long have you guys been together?"

I plopped my backpack down and pulled out my Fang piccie that I always sleep with, and put it on the dresser at the end of the bed. I reminded myself that I was absolutely secure with Fang, and didn't in the least have a problem with another girl having the hots for him. He was mine, mine, mine, and he knew it. "Well, I don't know exactly what you want to know about him. We met while I was living in England, and he came out to school here so we could be together. I live in Seattle, so it's only a few hours away. We've been going together for almost a year now."

"Wow, romantic," she said, assuming a lotus position on her bed. "Is he pretty good in bed?"

"Huh?" I asked, abso-bloody-lutely stunned. I thought for a minute that I had imagined what she said, but she giggled at me.

"He's got that quiet, brooding look that screams 'stallion in bed.' So is he?"

OK, you know full well that Fang and I haven't . . .

you know. I mean, I was planning on it for the cruise, but now that's all gone to hell, but I decided, looking at JWAE's smug look, that I would rather die from one of Brother's gawd-awful medieval tortures than tell her Fang and I hadn't done it.

"Oh, yeah. He's very hunkable."

"Thought so," she said, grabbing a pillow and hugging it. "How many times have you done it with him?"

My jaw dropped. I couldn't stop it; it just fell on the floor. "I don't . . . I can't believe . . . you know, that's kind of a personal question," I finally managed to stammer out.

"That many, huh?" She wiggled her eyebrows at me. "What's your favorite posish?"

This time my jaw didn't drop, but my brain stopped for a few seconds while I tried to get past her asking such highly personal questions. "Um. The normal one."

"Traditional, eh? Do you like to be the one in charge? Or does he?"

My brain had completely shut down at that point. I tried to look blasé, like I talked about sex with Fang every single day. "Well, he always asks me what I want to do," I said truthfully (only I wasn't talking about hooking up).

"So he's into being dominated, eh? Interesting," she said, looking thoughtful. "Do you guys do role playing games?"

"Um. Well, there's a really cool online pirate game that Fang likes. . . ."

"No," she said, making a funny face and shaking her

head like I was too dense for words. "Sex games! Do you guys get into role playing? I'm really into that, and I thought we could exchange scenarios—"

"I have to use the bathroom," I said, jumping off the bed. "Like, right now."

"Oh. OK. It's right through there. It's kind of small, but all the dorm baths are."

I took as long as I could in the tiny bathroom without making it seem like I had the trots or anything. When I came out I told her really quickly that I was majorly tired and had a big day and would go to bed right away. She tried to slip in a few more smutty questions, but I slapped my headphones on and just smiled a lot, and managed to get her off my back by climbing into bed right away. I lay there for *hours* wide-awake, because when was the last time you went to bed at nine? But I couldn't move because I was pretending to be asleep.

Fortunately she left me alone the next morning to go to a sunrise yoga class, so I ate the Pop-Tarts I'd brought with me (you can't go wrong with a PT for breffie, say I), poked around the dorm room without being too snoopy, then gathered up my stuff and trotted downstairs to some benches so I could meet Fang.

He bought me a latte and we talked together for an hour before he had to go off to his classes.

"What classes are you going to sit in on?" he asked as we walked (hands: held—major squeeage).

"Oh, there's a freshman 'physics for idiots' class that I

thought I'd check out first, then maybe one of the chem labs."

"Freshman physics?" Fang asked, giving me a smile that made me so happy I smiled back at him, which made us both stop and smile at each other for a while until someone yelled at us for blocking the door. He pulled me aside so the crabby person could go past. "That's kind of tame for you, isn't it? I thought you did all those advanced classes so you could skip the freshman classes."

"Some, but not all, and yeah, it is tame, but it's the only physics class offered in the morning. There's a really cool quantum mechanics one, but it's not until this afternoon, and I have to leave by noon in order to catch the train back."

"Have I told you how much I appreciate your giving up one of those posh unis to be here with me?" he asked, his gorgeous brown eyes all melty as they smiled at me. I got goose bumps up and down my arms just looking at him.

"Well, it's only fair. You gave up college in England for me," I answered, trying to look cool and sophisticated, and not at all like I was about to turn into a great big puddle of Emily if Fang didn't stop looking so snogarific. "Are you sure just one kiss—"

He laughed and hugged me, saying softly into my ear, "Love, there's nothing I want to do more than kiss the breath right out of you. No, I tell a lie; there is something else I want to do, but since we can't, I'm going to go into my class and you're going to go to yours."

I'd like to say that I left him like a mature, in-control sort of person, but the sad truth, Hol, is that it took me five whole minutes before I could get my knees stiff enough so I could walk.

"His super knee-melting powers seem to be getting stronger," I said to myself on the train a few hours later, as I was heading back to Seattle. "It used to take me only two minutes to recover from being around him."

The woman sitting next to me gave me a weird look.

"Sorry," I said. "Just talking to myself. I don't normally do that, because, you know, people who do that are too creepy for words, but I was with my boyfriend earlier today, and he's so amazingly nummy, he makes me brain go all wonky for a bit. I call it the Fang Effect, but don't worry—it's not permanent."

The woman nodded, muttered something I didn't quite hear, and left. I guess she thought I was strange or something, which just goes to show you how powerful the Fang Effect is.

Anyhoo, the classes I sat in on were fine. Pretty boring, but fine, and now I'm all registered and stuff, so yay! College at the beginning of October! I can't wait!

Enough of Em, Em, Em. What's up with Hol, Hol, Hol?

Huggers!
~Em

Subject: So?
From: Emster@seattlegrrl.com
To: Fbaxter@doormouse.ca
Date: June 27, 2005 1:11 pm

How is your spleen?

Emily (concerned)

Subject: Re: So?
From: Emster@seattlegrrl.com
To: Fbaxter@doormouse.ca
Date: June 27, 2005 1:17 pm

> *My spleen is fine. So are my liver, my gallbladder, and*
> *both my upper and lower intestines. My heart misses*
> *you, though.*

OK, that is just about the most romantic thing you've ever said to me, and that includes the time you said I was your best friend. (I still get a bit weepy when I remember that. It was just the nicest, most sweetest thing to say . . . Oh, poop. Gotta find Kleenex. BRB.)

I'm back. Anyway, take care of all your internal stuff. The cruise is only a week away, and I know you won't be able to do a lot of the strenuous stuff, but I don't want you to be sick during the cruise.

Tell your heart mine misses it, as well.

Major lovies,
Emily

Subject: Re: Bleargh
From: Emster@seattlegrrl.com
To: Devonator@skynetcomm.com
Date: June 30, 2005 8:58 am

> looked like hell, but he says the meds are helping, so
> stop worrying. Fang's a strong bloke. He's not going
> to cork off anytime soon. It was great seeing you,
> too, and thanks, my head is just fine now, so you can
> stop worrying that you ruined my trip. Besides, I'm
> kind of getting used to being puked on or having my
> head bashed in whenever I'm around you.

Hey! I only *once* bashed your head in! There's no "getting used to it" at all about that. The barfing is something else (not going there, thank you very much).

I'm glad you're home again, although I wish you could have stayed here longer. Fang and I are thinking that maybe we could do a trip to England next year, so who knows? Maybe we'll all be able to get together again.

> Thanks for sending me the pictures of all the clothes
> you bought for your cruise. Erm . . . I've been on a
> couple of cruises with Mum and don't think I've ever
> had to have thermal underwear and hiking boots, but
> you don't find a big need for those things in the Ca-
> ribbean.

All right, Mr. Smarty-pants. You know full well this cruise is going up to Alaska, not somewhere warm and nummy. Fang is really excited about seeing all the wildlife and some big glacier or something. Me, I'd rather go to Mexico like Dru did, but that stupid time-share place only had this cruise to pick from.

It'll be fun. I think. OK, so my idea of fun isn't sitting around being cold in Alaska, but Fang will be there, and that'll make it wonderful.

Do you appreciate just how self-sacrificing I'm being here? I sure hope someone does. And I want some of those karma points that Bess is always going on about, because I really did have my heart set on a suntan and tropical drinks and snorkeling and stuff.

Hugsies and all that,
Saint Emily

Subject: Spleen check!
From: Emster@seattlegrrl.com
To: Fbaxter@doormouse.ca
Date: June 30, 2005 2:24 pm

Is it OK?

Kissies,
Emily

Subject: Re: I hate my life
From: Emster@seattlegrrl.com
To: Hollyberry@britsahoy.co.uk
Date: July 1, 2005 9:17 pm

> *Everything is horrible here. I asked Mum if I could*
> *move in with Peter, and she said no, that he had his*
> *own problems, and didn't need to have a sister bol-*
> *locking everything up. We had a bit of a knock-down*
> *(but without the actual hitting), and I left the house*
> *for a few hours. When I came back Mum had the po-*
> *lice round, telling them she thought I was going to*
> *do something stupid like cut myself.*

Oh, man. Oh, man, oh, man, oh, man. Tell me you're not into cutting! That is just so freaky. I mean, here I am, so totally antipain I just can't imagine wanting to purposely do something like that to let everyone know that you're not happy with them.

OK, I'm going to tell you something that only Fang knows. Well, and Brother. I haven't even told Dru about this, but I will tell you because I think you'd understand.

You remember how depressed I was last year after we came home from England? Actually, Brother was as well, 'cause you know how much he loved being there, too. Anyway, that week you didn't hear from me was really bad. I was *so* majorly depressed. I was happy to see Dru and stuff, but it was like I didn't belong here anymore. I missed you, and Fang, and Devon, and everyone back there in Piddlesville, and I ended up staying in bed for a couple of days.

So there I was late one night, and I had been crying a lot, and was miserable, and wasn't sure Fang was going to be able to come to BC to go to college, and I really thought that since everything was so horrible, I might as well be dead or something.

Brother knocked on my door. I was a bit surprised, because he'd been going to bed really early the last few days, but he came in and looked horrible. He looked like my grandfather did before he died—all old and gray and kind of . . . deflated. Even his hair horn was lying flat, like it was too much trouble for it to stick up like it normally does.

"Your mother says you're not eating or sleeping. She's worried about you," Brother said, his eyes all red and tired-looking.

I went all puddly just thinking about how miserable I was, and how miserable I knew Brother was (Mom and Bess didn't mind coming home so much, but I knew Brother really hated to leave England), so I didn't say anything; I just nodded and grabbed the Kleenex box.

Brother didn't say anything either for a few minutes. He just stood there and looked at me; then he finally rubbed his hand over his face and said, "Do you feel like your heart has been torn out of your chest, too?"

I nodded again. "Yeah."

"Everything seems strange and out of focus?"

I swallowed back a huge lump in my throat. "And nothing matters."

He nodded this time. "I hate feeling like this."

A tear rolled down my cheek. "Me too."

He stood all uncomfortable-looking in my doorway. "So what are we going to do about it?"

"I don't know," I said, crying some more. "I don't know what to do to stop feeling this way. Everything is so awful."

He nodded again, rubbing his hand through his hair. "I think we need to do something to memorialize our time in England."

"Memorialize?" I asked, blowing my nose.

"Something to mark how we've been changed by our year in England. Something that will remind us always of the time we spent there, and the friends we made."

I frowned, trying to figure out what he was talking about. "Like what?"

He squinted at my clock radio. "What time is it?"

I looked. "Almost two A.M."

"Get dressed," he said, going out my door. "Meet me downstairs."

"What? Brother, what—"

I didn't want to yell after him because Mom and Bess were asleep (that was before Bess moved out), but I was worried about him. He seemed as upset as I was, and although I couldn't possibly be any more miserable, the thought that he might do something stupid had me pulling on a pair of jeans and a tee. I didn't bother with makeup, though, and you have to know that shows you just how depressed I really was.

Brother didn't say anything when I went downstairs. He just opened the front door and went out to the car. I figured I'd better follow him in case he was going to try to run himself over with the car or something.

Well, he didn't try to run himself over. He just got in the car. I figured Mom would want me to keep an eye on him, so I got in too, wondering what was going on.

"Um. You're not going to crash us into a tree or something?" I asked as he left the neighborhood and headed toward downtown Seattle.

"Don't be ridiculous. Death never solved anything."

"Then where are we going?"

"You'll see."

I shrugged to myself and watched all the lights flicker past as he got on the freeway. It was a Tuesday night, so you wouldn't expect there to be a ton of people out, but there were. At least, until we got off the freeway and headed into downtown. Then the streets were empty, which was kinda freaky, to be honest.

"Um," I said, when I noticed that Brother was heading for Pioneer Square. "Does Mom know we're going here? 'Cause she told me never to come here late at night."

"Your mother doesn't know anything about this," Brother said.

My eyes widened at that. Mom and Brother never

keep stuff from each other. They can't even keep Christmas presents a secret.

"OK," I said slowly, wondering if he was taking us to be killed by drug-crazed street people. (I know, it sounds stupid now, but you see what you think at two A.M. when you're out on empty, freaky streets in Pioneer Square.)

He cruised up and down the streets slowly, evidently looking for something. All I saw were a couple of people huddled in unhappy lumps on some benches, a few others scrounging around a big garbage can, a bunch of closed stores with big metal bars on their windows, a couple of bars that were just closing up for the night, a few sex shops with more iron bars and big glaring neon lights, a twenty-four-hour tattoo shop with lots of pictures in the windows, and an adult theater that had a few guys outside it (ew!). Brother found a pay parking lot that was empty, and pulled into the spot nearest the street.

I got out of the car, wondering if Brother had finally flipped. He was starting to scare me, but I didn't want to tell him that in case he really had gone insane. A calm, insane Brother would be much easier to get back into the car than a wild, irrational, insane Brother, right? Well, that's what I was thinking, anyhoo.

Brother headed for the sex shop. I started mentally planning my phone call to Mom to tell on him when he grabbed my arm and pulled me close as a couple of street guys jumped out of an alley.

"Stay close, and don't say anything," he warned in a low voice.

We walked quickly past the street guys, one of whom waved a bottle in a paper bag at us and said something really rank (not going to repeat it). To my relief we hurried past the sex shop, but my jaw just about hit the pavement when Brother stopped in front of the tattoo shop, pushing me through the door before following me.

I blinked like mad in the bright lights of the shop. There were a couple of chairs set in front of a low table, and beyond it a big chair, the kind dentists have, only without the spit sink. The walls were absolutely floor-to-ceiling with pictures of tats and stuff, and at the rear there was piercing equipment.

I looked at Brother. "You want us to get tats?"

He took off his coat. "Can you think of a better way to immortalize our time in England?"

"But . . . I wanted to get a tat two years ago and you said you'd die rather than let me mutilate myself that way!"

"I've changed my mind," he said grimly, turning when a woman with bright yellow (and I mean yellow, not blond) hair came out of a back room. "My daughter and I would like tattoos."

"Cool," the woman said, waving her hands around at the wall. "What appeals to you?"

"Do you have any Pict designs?" Brother asked. To my surprise, the woman nodded.

"We get a number of requests for tribal art. I have a few designs here." She handed him a thin notebook. "If you need more, I can do some research and hunt down something else."

Brother sat down on a shiny plastic couch and started looking through the book. The woman, who said her name was Gigi, asked me what I wanted.

"Well," I said, still kind of stunned by the whole thing. "I think I want a heart. Because I feel like I left my heart behind in England."

"Awww," Gigi said, making a sad face as she patted me on my shoulder. "Long-distance relationships are tough. My lover is in Austria. I won't see her for another three months."

"I may never get to see my boyfriend again," I said, getting a bit teary.

She tipped her head and eyed me as I did the Kleenex thing (I hate crying in front of people). "How about a Celtic-knot heart? Those are very pretty and delicate, and yet can show the intricacies and difficulties of relationships."

"That sounds good."

I sat next to Brother to look through the notebook she gave me, finally picking a design I liked. (It's a Celtic-heart knot, really detailed and pretty—I'll show it to you if you get to come out here for Christmas.) Brother chose a twirled knot that was supposed to be a representation of warrior strength.

"Are you sure you want to do this?" I asked him in a

whisper as Gigi took the papers Brother and I signed (saying we wouldn't sue them or anything like that) and started prepping the tat gun.

"It's a way for me to physically commemorate my time in England," he said, looking determined. "How about you?"

"Yeah. This is good," I said, suddenly feeling a little bit better. I know it sounds weird, but he was right— getting a tat was kind of a way to recognize how my life had changed in England. It wouldn't make life any less sucky if Fang didn't get to come to BC, but somehow it was important that I do something to show how much I'd changed.

Brother went first. I knew exactly where I wanted my tat—on my left hip. Brother decided to get his on his chest, near his heart.

"Mom's going to see it," I said as he sat in Gigi's dentist chair. "She's going to freak. You know she doesn't like tats."

"I have no doubt that I'll hear about it for years," he agreed. "But some things are worth a sacrifice."

He leaned back so Gigi could work on him. She shaved a small spot on his chest with a little razor, then swabbed him down with alcohol a couple of times.

I watched as she set out little cups of dye (Brother's tat was just going to be blue, but mine was done in reds and oranges), and a couple packages of needles, and the tat gun.

"This is a thermal transfer," Gigi said as she peeled

off a bit of paper and stuck it on the shaved spot. "It transfers the design you picked."

"Cool," I said as she pulled the paper off. It was like a purplish temporary tattoo.

"Ready?" she asked Brother as she pulled on a pair of rubber gloves.

He took a deep breath and nodded. I stood at his feet and smiled at him.

"For England," he said, all dramatic-like. I nodded and gritted my teeth as the woman smeared a little ointment on the transfer, then picked up the tat gun and started slowly drawing in the outline of Brother's tat.

I'll say this for my father—he didn't scream or pass out or anything embarrassing like that. He looked like he was going to ralph the first few minutes, but after that he settled down and just looked like Mom was making him eat brussels sprouts.

Gigi did me in a small curtained-off area where people who want tats in embarrassing spots can have some privacy.

"Would you like me to come with you?" Brother asked, slipping his shirt on over the bandage Gigi had put over his new tat.

"Hello! I'm going to be in my undies!" I said, giving him a look.

"And of course, I don't see you run through the house in your underwear at least five times a day," he said with one of those father looks that made me think he was feeling better, too.

My tat went pretty fast. It only took about forty minutes, and didn't hurt much at all. Well, OK, it did, but only at first, then my left side kind of went numb or something. I had thought of having the tat right on my hip bone, but Gigi said that would hurt a lot, and suggested a spot on the side of my hip.

"If you have it right here, it will be hidden by your panties unless you want it to be seen," Gigi said when I explained that I didn't want a tat that just anyone could see. She touched a spot on the side of my hip. "Thongs will show it off, but panties like you have on now will keep it secret until you want to reveal it."

"Do it," I told her, making the decision. Brother came and stood just outside the curtain a couple of times to ask if I was all right (which was kind of nice), and by the time Gigi was finished and put some ointment and a bandage on my hip, I was surprised to find that I wasn't very depressed anymore.

"Does yours hurt?" Brother asked as we stood on the sidewalk outside the shop.

"Yeah. Does yours?"

"Quite a surprising amount, to be honest."

We looked at each other.

"It's a good hurt, though, huh?" I asked.

"Very good," he agreed.

Brother never did tell Mom that I got a tat. He didn't outright lie to her, but he said he went to Seattle and got his tat, leaving out the fact that I was with him. I think she suspected something at first, because my hip was sore and stuff for a few days, but she never said anything, and I've been really careful to make sure it doesn't show when I run to the bathroom. Mom gave Brother hell for weeks, but you know, I have to give him props—he really had a good idea with the tats. Now whenever I see mine, I think about you, and Devon, and Fang, and everyone in England, and how much fun we've had, and how much I miss you all. Only instead of it being depressing, it's kind of a celebration.

I haven't explained it very well, have I? I'm sorry about that. It's kind of an emotional subject, but I wanted you to know that I understand how crappy you feel, and that if you want to do something to make a change in your life, there's lots of things you can do that aren't going to cause you pain or make your mom lock you away or anything. Well, OK, tattoos cause pain, but only for a little bit; then you have a really cool tat.

Fang is the only one who's seen my tat, but I'll show it to you when you come out here, because you're just as much a part of it as he is.

Big, big hugs, and lots of kisses.
~Em

You have a Chat Girl Instant Message. Click to receive it.

GonnaMarryFelix: Sigh.
GonnaMarryFelix: I'm bored.

Em=c^2: You could come over and help me pack.

GonnaMarryFelix: Oh, that sounds thrilling.

Em=c^2: Hey, I'm just trying to be helpful Saint Emily.

GonnaMarryFelix: Oh, yeah, saint, riiiiiight. I suppose I could come over and help you pack. It's not like I have anything else in my life to do.

Em=c^2: Mmm.

GonnaMarryFelix: You're not very chatty today.

Em=c^2: I'm trying to pack!

GonnaMarryFelix: You can't type and pack at the same time?

Em=c^2: Not when I have to type with one and a half hands. Fwah. Why did I buy so much stuff?

GonnaMarryFelix: Because you blew your whole graduation present at Eddie Bauer?

Em=c^2: I didn't blow the whole thousand. Only part of it.

GonnaMarryFelix: Em, honey, it took you, me, and Suky to carry everything you bought there. I mean, honestly, some of the stuff you bought! Yeah, I can see the Gore-Tex parka (I like the lavender one you got, but I still think the lime would have looked better with your coloring), and I understand about needing lots of sweaters and stuff, but did you really need to get those titanium boots?

Em=c^2: They're Titanium Ice Crushers, and yes, I did. You can't walk around on glaciers and stuff with just any boots, you know. You need special ice ones.

GonnaMarryFelix: But you bought two pairs!

Em=c^2: Well, I had to get some for Fang, too! I don't want to play on a glacier without him!

GonnaMarryFelix: It's July. How much ice is Alaska going to have?

Em=c^2: The cruise stuff says we're going to visit a big glacier, so it's probably there year-round.

GonnaMarryFelix: Why doesn't it melt in the summer?

Em=c^2: Do I look like I'm an iceberg expert?

GonnaMarryFelix: Hmm.

GonnaMarryFelix: I'm still bored.

Em=c^2: I thought you were going to come over and help me pack?

GonnaMarryFelix: I can if you want me to.

Em=c^2: It's OK. I'm almost done. Um. You don't think five suitcases is too much for a weeklong cruise, do you?

GonnaMarryFelix: Ahahahahahahahahahah.

Em=c^2: /me sighs.

GonnaMarryFelix: You're never going to fit that on the plane coming home.

Em=c^2: Ugh. I didn't think about that. OK. I need to consolidate. That can't be hard. I'll just unpack everything, lay it out, and repack only those things I absotively *have* to have.

GonnaMarryFelix: Bored, bored, bored.

GonnaMarryFelix: Boredy, boredy, boredy, bored, bored.

GonnaMarryFelix: I'll sing to you while you're repacking.

Em=c^2: Um. Maybe you ought to come over after all.

GonnaMarryFelix: Consolidating not going well?
Em=c^2: Well . . . now I have six suitcases.
GonnaMarryFelix: Super Packer Dru is on the way!

Chat Girl GonnaMarryFelix has left.

Subject: Re: What are you two doing up there?
From: Emster@seattlegrrl.com
To: Hwilliams@ewedub.edu
Date: July 2, 2005 8:54 pm

> *It sounds like you're training a troupe of moose to*
> *tap dance. I'm trying to finish up the first draft of this*
> *very important book. Would you and Dru mind tak-*
> *ing your dancing moose somewhere else until I'm*
> *done?*

Excuse me, strange person e-mailing me, do I know you? I'm very busy packing for my fabulous cruise in two days. There are no moose, dancing or otherwise, funny man. And someone needs to do some serious chilling out! Or better yet, go take your meds.

Emily the divine

Subject: You are a bad man!
From: Emster@seattlegrrl.com
To: Hwilliams@ewedub.edu
Date: July 2, 2005 9:00 pm

> *Good suggestion. Since I don't have any medication*
> *now, why don't you bring me some back from*
> *Canada? I suspect in order to survive the next four*
> *years I'm going to need a lot of Valium, so be sure to*
> *buy in bulk!*

I'm going to tell Mom you're trying to get me to buy you drugs! You're *so* going to be in trouble!

Em (still divine)

Subject: Hollycakes?
From: Emster@seattlegrrl.com
To: Hollyberry@britsahoy.co.uk
Date: July 2, 2005 10:18 pm

Hol? I haven't heard from you for a day. You OK? Dru and I are worried. She came over to help me pack (I'm down to three suitcases, woo-hoo!), and I was telling her that you're going through a really down time. I hope you don't mind that I told her, but she went bonkers when Felix signed up for the army. She had to go to a therapist and everything, and they put her on happy drugs for a bit because she really wigged out royally. So she knows how bad things can be.

Anyhoodles, we're worried. So let me know how you are.

Hugsies,
~Em

Subject: Re: T minus 2 and counting
From: Emster@seattlegrrl.com
To: Fbaxter@doormouse.ca
Date: July 2, 2005 10:27 pm

> *I'm fine, love. Just fine. You can stop checking with*
> *me five times a day. I like all the e-mails, but you*
> *don't have to worry about my spleen or anything*
> *else. The doc says as long as I'm careful, there should*
> *be no problem. Any word from Holly?*

I'm glad you're feeling better. No word on Holly. I'm worried.

Smoochums. Two more days to sheer and utter bliss!

Emily

Subject: Um . . . Hol?
From: Emster@seattlegrrl.com
To: Hollyberry@britsahoy.co.uk
Date: July 3, 2005 8:22 am

Hey, Holly. I know you probably don't want to e-mail anyone right now if you've gone all blue, but I'm really, really worried. Can you just let me know you're OK? Like, today? 'Cause I leave on my cruise tomorrow, and I'm not sure if the ship is going to have Internet or not.

Frowny, worried hugs and kisses,
~Em

Em=c^2: No e-mail from Holly.

GonnaMarryFelix: Uh-oh. You think she's done something?

Em=c^2: Don't know. But I'm worried. She was really down.

GonnaMarryFelix: You could call her house.

Em=c^2: Her mom would probably answer. And if I asked her if Holly is OK, and she didn't know Holly was all blues girl, then she'd know, and probably bug Holly to death.

GonnaMarryFelix: True. Maybe you shouldn't call, then.

Em=c^2: Think I'll e-mail Devon and see if he can go over to Holly's and make sure she's OK.

GonnaMarryFelix: Ooooh, smart idea!

Subject: Big favor
From: Emster@seattlegrrl.com
To: Devonator@skynetcomm.com
Date: July 3, 2005 8:28 am

I'm worried about Holly. I haven't heard from her for a couple of days, and the last e-mail I got said she was really depressed. Fang and I are leaving tomorrow for Alaska. Can you go check on her for me, please?

Major big-time smoochies!
~Em

Subject: Spleen: The Musical
From: Emster@seattlegrrl.com
To: Fbaxter@doormouse.ca
Date: July 3, 2005 9:16 am

> *like a smart idea to ask Dev to check, although I'm*
> *sure nothing has happened to Holly. She's got a*
> *pretty level head. I'm discontinuing spleen updates.*
> *Please consult the National Spleen Information Cen-*
> *tre for further details regarding general spleen health*
> *and well-being. The Fang chapter has closed its doors*
> *to all further inquiries.*

I'm your girlfriend! It's in my job description to be obsessed with the status of your near-exploding spleen!
Don't forget to pack all your mono meds.

Tomorrow can't get here fast enough! I can't wait to see you again!

Big fat kisses,
Emily

Em=c^2: I can't wait to see the cruise ship!

GonnaMarryFelix: You're gonna love it. The one Mom and I went on in Mexico was huge. Tons and tons of shops and nightclubs and stuff like that. They had a casino, too, but Mom wouldn't let me go in there.

Em=c^2: You weren't eighteen then. I am. So I can casino if I want! Yay!

GonnaMarryFelix: Yeah, that will be fun.

Em=c^2: I can't wait to see our cabin. I can't wait to sleep with Fang!

GonnaMarryFelix: What???? You're going to sleep with him? You didn't tell me that!

Em=c^2: I did too!

GonnaMarryFelix: You did not! I think I'd remember you saying something like that!

Em=c^2: I told you we were going to share a cabin, and that there would probably be only one bed in it because the reservations lady asked if I wanted one bed or two, and I said one.

GonnaMarryFelix: Omigod! I can't believe you're going to sleep with Fang!

Em=c^2: Sigh. Dru, I'm not going to sleep with him; I'm going to *sleep* with him.

GonnaMarryFelix: I know; you just told me. OMG!!!

Em=c^2: Sleep! We're going to sleep! Just sleep! He's got mono, remember?

GonnaMarryFelix: Oh. That's right. So you're not going to . . . you know?

Em=c^2: No. We're just going to sleep together.

GonnaMarryFelix: !!!

Em=c^2: Stop it; you're giving me a headache. Oooh, e-mail from Devon.

GonnaMarryFelix: What's he say?

Em=c^2: He's going to stop by Holly's house later tonight.

GonnaMarryFelix: Good. Let me know what he finds out.

Em=c^2: Oh, no!

GonnaMarryFelix: What?

Em=c^2: Now what am I going to do?

GonnaMarryFelix: About what?

Em=c^2: This is just horrible!

GonnaMarryFelix: What???

Em=c^2: Brother says I can only have two suitcases on an airplane!

GonnaMarryFelix: /me sighs.

GonnaMarryFelix: I'll be there in ten.

Em=c^2: Stupid airline rules. Meh!

Chat Girl GonnaMarryFelix has left.

Subject: re: Holly Update
From: Emster@seattlegrrl.com
To: Devonator@skynetcomm.com
Date: July 4, 2005 7:12 am

> *wasn't sure where she was, but when I called this*
> *morning, she said Hol was back, and she wasn't hurt.*
> *I'm going to stop by and try to see her today, al-*
> *though her mum didn't sound like she was going to*
> *be happy with company. But at least you can stop*
> *worrying that she's dead or something.*

Thank you so much, Devon. I really appreciate your checking on Holly for me. Did her mom say where she had been for the last two days? Did she go with her kinda BF? Or did she just go off on her own? I know she wanted to live with her brother, Peter, but her mom wouldn't let her. Maybe she went to stay with him?

Tell her I really miss her and I'm worried about her and stuff, and that I'll try to e-mail from the cruise ship.

Gotta run. I'm meeting Fang early, so we may do a little bit of shopping for him, since he doesn't have much glacier-wear.

Tons of hugs!
~Em

Subject: Emily & Fang: The World Tour—Day 1
From: emilyw@cruiseseattle.com
To: Dru@seattlegrrl.com
Date: July 5, 2005 11:38 am

Ahoy and avast! Belay that barnacle! And other ship-ish talk. I finally managed to get some time at the computer, although I had to wait until a talk on seabirds before the old ones would leave it alone.

Man, Dru, I'm telling you—old people are mean!

But I'm doing that foreshadowing thing Mom always rants about whenever she reads a mystery.

BTW, Fang and I aren't married. Just in case one of the old ones knows someone you know. They think we're married, but we've told them we're not. But will they believe us? Nooo.

Wait, I'd better start at the beginning or you'll just end up with that funny look you get on your face whenever you're confused. The beginning—I met Fang in Seattle, where he'd come down from Vancouver so we could get on the cruise ship together. Mom and Brother wanted to see us off and stuff, but I did my usual polite-but-firm bit with them to gently let them know that although I appreciated it, I really would prefer to savor every minute I had with Fang.

"I'd rather have flounder stuffed under my fingernails," I yelled at Brother when he tried to pull the old "you can't go unless I can see you off" business. As if!

So I met Fang alone at the train station in Seattle, and

after I was finished kissing all the parts of him that I was allowed to kiss, we took a taxi down to the pier to do the getting-on-board-the-cruise-ship thing.

"Wow, look at that one," I said, pointing to a huge, huge, *huge*, massive white ship that was docked. "The *Sun Princess*. That ship is huge—it has to be at least a block long. Cool. Is that our ship?"

"I don't think so," Fang said, looking at the cruise info I got after I sent in my freebie cruise coupon. "This says our ship's name is . . . *Bob*."

"What?" I asked, looking at another huge cruise ship as the taxi zipped down the waterfront. "Oooh. Carnival. I've heard of them. What do you mean, our ship's name is *Bob*. *Bob* what? *Bob Marley? Bobbin' Along?*"

"Just *Bob*." Fang said, showing me the cruise confirmation letter. I looked. Sure enough, it had listed under ship name, "*Bob*."

"Huh. Must be short for something. Look, that one is called the *Sun Dancer!* That's a great ship name. Omigod, I can see a swimming pool on it! I hope that one is ours!"

"I don't think so, Em," Fang said, reading the letter. "This says that Cruise Seattle is a company known for its small cruise ships that can go places the big ones can't."

"Oh," I said, looking at yet another mammoth cruise ship. "Well, smaller would be OK."

"Pier sixty-nine," the taxi guy said, pulling up to a place with a blue-and-white awning set up. "Cruise Seattle is just over there."

"Cool. Thanks." We grabbed our bags (I don't know how you got everything of mine into two, but I wish you'd fly up to Alaska to help me repack it, because I have a really bad feeling the sea air is making everything expand) and dragged them over to the awning, which turned out to be a hospitality area. The Cruise Seattle people gave us a couple of grizzly-bear pins (why? Who knows!), checked us in, and took our bags.

"You have three hours before the ship sails," the checking-in guy said. "Feel free to take in some of the sights of lovely Seattle while you wait."

"You wanna be tourists?" I asked Fang, not really wanting to sit around the hospitality area that long.

"Sure. You can show me everything you didn't show me the last time I was here."

We ended up going to Pike Place Market and hanging out at the Starbucks, just yakking about everything—Fang's classes, his father (who is being a pain again), Holly, and all sorts of other stuff. I tried to get him to tell me how his spleen was, but he refused to even talk about it, which I thought was a bit mean. A little later, when we were walking along the row of flower vendors, and trying to avoid everyone on the sidewalk who were watching a Kiddie Fourth of July parade, Fang suddenly pulled me over to an out-of-the-way corner and gave me a weird look.

"Emily, I have something I want to say," he said, all serious-like.

"Omigod, it's your spleen," I said, racing around him

so I could get at his side. "Has it exploded? Should I call nine-one-one? I knew we should have just waited on the dock rather than trekked all over the city!"

Fang looked upward for a minute, just like Brother does when he's pretending to be put-upon. "It's not my spleen. My spleen is fine. *I'm* fine, Em, so you can stop trying to unbutton my shirt in front of everyone."

"Well, if it's not your spleen, then what's the matter?"

"Nothing's the matter," he said, the weird look coming back over his face.

"Then why do you look so uncomfortable? Something has to be wrong, Fang. You look like you stepped on a nail, or haven't gone to the bathroom in days, or like you're one of those guys the witch-hunters tortured by putting really big slabs of cement and stuff on them."

Fang started laughing, but before I could ask what he thought was so funny, he put his hand over my mouth. "I have something I want to say to you."

"What?" I asked, my voice kind of muffled because of his fingers across my lips. "Does it have anything to do with your mono? Because if you're not feeling well enough to go on the—"

"I'm fine!" he said, his voice getting a little loud even though he was still laughing. "It has nothing to do with my health."

I thought for a minute. "If this has something to do with me getting you those glacier boots, then I'm just going to la-la-la you and not listen to you again, because it was my graduation bucks to be spent however I wanted, and I wanted you to have really cool glacier hiking boots, too—"

"No!" Fang said, his voice getting even louder. "I like the boots! That's not what I wanted to say!"

I was worried now. You know what guys are like when it comes to money. Half of them want everything you have; the other half won't let you buy them anything. Men! I figured I'd better reassure Fang that I wasn't going to treat him like he was a boy toy by buying him stuff all the time. "Good, because some guys get a little weird if their GF has more money than they have, but this wasn't really money. It was my graduation present from my family, not money I made, so it doesn't count, not really."

"Emily, if you'd just listen to me—"

"So if you're worried that I'm going to spend the rest of the trip buying you things, don't. For one, I'm broke, and for another, I know all about guys and their pride—"

"I just wanted to tell you how much I love you, and how proud I am of you!" he yelled.

Several people standing nearby buying flowers turned around to look at us. I stared at Fang, surprised by the fact that he yelled at me; then I whooped and jumped on him and kissed his face all over again.

"That's so romantic, bellowing it out like that," I told him as soon as I was through with the kissing.

"Well, I didn't actually intend on informing everyone at the market, but it is true," he said, tucking a loose strand of my hair behind my ear. I went all melty at that, and had to make an effort to stiffen up my knees. "I'm very proud of you for graduating and getting into Carlyle, and grateful that you'd give up a better college just so we can be together."

"Don't be silly," I said, pretending there was something on his shirt so I could do the GF move and brush it off. "Of course I wanted to go to Carlyle. And they have a good physics program, so it's no sacrifice."

"I want to give you something," he said, the odd look coming back. "But I don't want you to think it means I expect any sort of commitment above what you are comfortable with."

"A present?" I asked, getting excited (you know how I love surprise presies!). "Oooh! Want to see!"

He pulled a tiny little box out of his pocket and held it out to me.

"That looks like a ring box," I said, major big goose bumps suddenly running wild on me, zinging up and down my arms and back.

He opened it up to show me a pretty ring with a blue stone set in a circle. "It belonged to my gran. She gave it to me a few weeks before she passed on, telling me to give it to the girl who captured my heart."

"Oh, God," I said, instantly going from happy, excited Em to weepy, melty Em. "That is the most romantic thing!"

"You don't have to wear it if you don't want to," he said, his eyes making him look just like a puppy that doesn't know if you're going to pet it or not. "I know you are attached to the ring Dev gave you—"

I yanked off the friendship ring Devon gave me and stuffed it into my bra (my other hand is still too swollen to wear any jewelry), holding out my good hand to him. "You can put it on," I told him, giving him my absolute best smile.

He plucked the ring out of the box and looked at my hand, hesitating. "Erm . . . which finger do you want it on?"

I looked at my hand. My middle finger had the marks of Dev's ring, but it seemed somehow wrong to put Fang's ring there. Dev was a friend, and his ring was offered in friendship. Fang was more than just a friend, though, so it was only right that his ring should be put on a special finger.

"Whichever one you want," I said, holding my breath for a minute to see what he would do.

"We'll try this one, then," he said, sliding it onto my ring finger. I screamed happily, flung myself on him again (being careful to watch out for his spleen), and kissed his face all over. Not that it was a strain or anything.

"Don't worry; I don't think we're engaged or anything," I said, laughing at the worried look on his face. "Dru has cornered wedding insanity." And stop giving the computer that look; you know full well that it's true!

"I'm just so happy that you'd give me something that belonged to your grandma. That's so sweet!"

"Well," he said, giving me a slow Fang smile, the one that makes my stomach feel all warm. "It's no pair of Titanium Ice Crusher boots, but I thought you'd like it all the same."

We spent the rest of the time poking around the market, with me doing the I-have-a-new-ring hand thing everywhere we went. It got me into a bit of trouble—we were in the Asian food store in the market, and I was waving my hand around a lot to make sure the girl behind the counter saw it, and I ended up knocking over a bunch of stuff from the shelf behind me.

"Eek," I shouted as a bag of rice fell from an upper shelf and exploded next to me. That knocked down a bottle of vinegar, which broke all over the floor. "Oh, man, I'm so sorry. Here, I'll pay for that—"

We got out of there really quickly after that, but we both had bits of rice everywhere. Fang bought me a small bouquet of carnations (my fave!) and we shared an elephant ear at the bakery, then headed back down to the pier so we could get on the ship.

"Welcome back, Fang and Emily," the cruise guy, whose name was actually Guy, said, smiling at us until he noticed we weren't wearing our grizzly-bear pins. "We're just about to start boarding. If you'd like a refreshment until then, please help yourselves. And don't be shy about meeting some of your fellow passengers. Almost everyone is here."

"Um," I said, turning to smile at everyone in the waiting area. I blinked a couple of times, like that would help, but it didn't. "Our fellow passengers?"

"Welcome! Are you with the Silver Puget Audubon group?" asked an old lady with yellowy-white hair, wearing a pale yellow sweatshirt and pants. She frowned at a clipboard (also pale yellow). "Guy said your names were Fang and Emily? I don't see you on the list."

"Uh," I said, backing up slowly as I looked at everyone else who was standing around waiting to get on the ship. They were all old, Dru. I mean *old!* Three of them had walkers, two were in wheelchairs, and the rest looked like . . . well, like really, really old people. "There's a mistake," I said, turning back to Guy. "We're supposed to be on the cruise to Alaska."

"Yes, that's right," he said.

"But," I said, jerking my head toward the oldsters, "you said that almost all the passengers were here, but all I see are . . . um . . . elderlyish people."

"Yes," Guy said, smiling and nodding. "The Silver Audubon group has reserved most of the ship for its members, but we had one available cabin, which is why you were allowed to pick this popular date, rather than waiting for off-peak season, as is traditional with our promotional giveaways."

"So there's just them and us?" I asked, not even wanting to imagine what it was going to be like around the pool. Old people in Speedos—ick!

"That is correct. You'll find the Auduboners an interesting group to sail with—they are extremely knowl-edgeable about bird life."

"But . . . they're all old," I said, leaning forward so I could whisper to the guy (I didn't want everyone hearing).

"Yes, that's why they call themselves Silver," Guy whispered back, then stood up and smiled over my shoulder. "And here are our last two guests! Welcome back! It's a delight to have you sailing with us again."

"Oh, man," I said to Fang as I stepped back so two old ladies could check in. "We're going to be on the Metamucil ship!"

Fang smiled and brushed at my shoulder. "It'll be all right, love. We'll still be together, and it might be nice traveling with people who know a lot about the birds we'll be seeing."

"But . . ." I said, wanting to bawl over my horrible luck, but knowing it would sound too spoiled for words. So I just shut up and rubbed the stone on the ring Fang had given me on my shirt, so it would look all sparkly.

"That rice got everywhere," Fang said, brushing my other shoulder.

"Rice?" a woman behind him said, turning around to look at us. Her eyes went from the rice Fang was pick-ing out of my hair to me polishing my ring, then nar-rowed at the small bouquet of flowers I had stuck in my purse. "Newlyweds!" she shrieked. "We have newly-weds with us!"

Everyone—and I do mean everyone—turned to look at us.

"Omigod! No! We're not married!" I said quickly. "My boyfriend gave me his grandmother's ring today, and I was showing it off and hit a bag of rice, and it went all over, and the flowers are just because he's sweet—this is him, by the way; doesn't he look sweet?—and although we're madly in love and stuff, we're not married. We're not even engaged. I have a friend who is, though. But we're not."

"Em," Fang said quietly, smiling at everyone as they clustered around us.

"I'm babbling, aren't I?" I asked through my teeth.

"Yes."

"Not married?" The troublemaker woman, the one who started it all (her name, I found out later, is Edith. That is *such* a troublemaker name!), frowned at us, then looked back at Guy. "I thought you said there was just one empty cabin?"

"Yes, that's right. Fang and Emily have cabin thirteen."

"They're cohabitating?" someone else asked, sounding all shocked and stuff. "On our trip? Margie, did you hear? Those two young people will be fornicating on our trip! Without the benefit of marriage."

"Oh, for Pete's sake, people!" I said, putting my hands on my hips and giving Margie and her twit of a husband a good, solid glare. "Get with the times! This is 2005, not 1905! People take cruises together all the time! And not that it's any of your business, but Fang and I will not be hooking up on this trip."

"Hooking up?" a really old guy said in a creaky voice.

He had hearing aids on, though, so I won't make fun of him for repeating what I said.

"Yeah, you know . . . getting together. Sex!" I said, when the oldsters looked confused.

Several people gasped. Fang groaned and closed his eyes.

"So you can all just stop worrying about that, because Fang can't do that."

The men all looked at Fang and nodded.

"Thanks, Em," Fang said in an odd, choked voice.

"So young to be affected," one woman said to another. They both shook their heads sadly.

"Vern, did you bring your Viagra?" A woman who looked kind of like my grandma elbowed a tall, thin guy.

I suddenly realized why Fang was looking embarrassed. "Oh, no! No, he doesn't need that! Fang doesn't have . . . you know, thingie problems. I mean, I don't know from firsthand experience, but I know him, and he'd tell me if he did. You'd tell me, wouldn't you, Fang? See? He would tell me. So it's not that. I'm sure he can do anything he wants to do perfectly well. Probably better than well, if his kissing is anything to go by! Although I haven't been able to kiss him lately, either, except on the face, which everyone knows doesn't really count. Anyway, it's just that he's been sick, and he isn't allowed to."

"Love, you're not really helping," Fang said. I squeezed his hand to let him know I was going to fix everything.

"He's been sick?" someone asked. "What kind of sick? Something contagious?"

"Well, I'm not going to tell you that," I said, giving the man who had asked a really firm look. "That's like an invasion of Fang's privacy! Sheesh! There're laws and stuff!"

"What did she say?" a woman in the back asked.

"She refuses to tell us what the young man is sick with. I say we vote them off the island," a short little bald man said.

"Someone has been watching way too much TV," I said to him. "We have tickets and everything. I *won* this cruise!"

"Good afternoon, everyone! It's a pleasure to have the Silver Auduboners back with us again." A big, burly man in a white shirt and jeans appeared behind everyone and smiled a really big smile. "How is everyone on this lovely Fourth of July?"

"Captain Jack! We're going to die," someone said as the entire group did an about-face and swarmed him.

"What?" The guy, who was the captain of the ship, looked a little surprised. "Not you, Melba. You'll outlive us all!"

"That young man is deathly ill with some horrible contagious disease, and he'll give it to us all," the (evil) oldster named Melba said, pointing at my dear, sweet, so-not-evil Fang.

"They're probably trying to go to Canada to get those

illegal medical treatments," Vern the Viagra guy said.

Everyone nodded.

"What's this?" Captain Jack asked, pushing his way forward.

"Hey! I've been to Canada for medical treatments," I said, holding up my cast. "They are very nice there, so don't be slamming them. And Fang lives there now! He's English."

"Damned foreigner," someone said. I glared at everyone, trying to pick out who said it.

"Perhaps I could have a word with you?" Captain Jack asked Fang.

"Stay here, Em," Fang said as the captain waved him toward a stack of wooden crates.

"I could help," I pointed out.

He smiled and gave my fingers a squeeze before letting go of my hand. "I know. But I think I can handle this on my own."

"Don't tell him anything," I yelled out after him as he went to join the captain. "No one has a right to know every little thing about you! You have a right to privacy!"

I turned back to confront a bunch of really old faces.

"You people need to get a grip," I told them all, then went to stand by the entrance of the hospitality area, ignoring the babble of conversation behind me.

OK, way longer story than I intended, too long to make short, but still, long story short: We got on the ship. Fang told the captain what he was sick with, and since there is no way for him to infect the oldsters (not without him snogging them, and that's just something that is way off the ew meter), the captain couldn't stop us from coming along on the trip.

The first day was pretty good, other than . . . Gah! I have to go. One of the evil elderly has complained about me hogging the computer, and Sam the first mate just told me I have to get off it.

More as soon as I can get back to the 'puter.

Hugs!
~Em

Subject: E & F: The World Tour—Day 2
From: emilyw@cruiseseattle.com
To: Dru@seattlegrrl.com
Date: July 6, 2005 9:18 pm

Man, I hate old people. OK, I don't really hate all old people. But I sure hate a couple of them! I wish this was a TV show and I could vote some people off the ship, because I'll tell you who would be the first to be thrown overboard: Melba and Vern! Gah!

Deep breath, Emily . . . OK. I'm calm again. I had a yoga class this morning, and Polly, the girl doing the class (who is also the one who runs the gift stand, and she helps clean the cabins, too) told me I need to de-stress by breathing properly. So I'm "in with the good air" in one side of my nose, and "out with the stress" out the other side.

Anyhoo, you probably don't want to hear me complain about the old people. So I won't. We're almost up to Alaska now, at the northern part of British Columbia. It's pretty woodsy and stuff, not a lot to see, although you wouldn't know that from these old birders (that's what they call themselves—Fang and I had a good snicker about that). Every time someone spots a bird, they run to that side of the ship and peer at it with their binoculars. I'm like, "It's a bird! Big deal."

Fang is having a good time, though. He actually likes the bird people.

"They just have a different focus than us, love," he told me last night as we were getting ready for bed. Or trying to, since our cabin is really small. "To them, the whole purpose of this trip is to see new species."

"Yeah, well, I don't care what they do so long as they leave us alone," I grumbled, then felt bad because this was our romantic cruise and I was in a pissy mood.

"You liked seeing the whales," Fang pointed out as he grabbed his jammies and toothbrush, stepped over where my bags stuck out from under my bed (the only storage spot), and headed for our teensy, tiny bathroom.

"Yeah, but they're cool. They're not some silly little birds."

"Tolerance, love. It takes all kinds."

"You sound so like Brother," I told the bathroom door as he closed it behind him, but I didn't mind, not really. We were together, and even if the ship was full of ancient ones who went gaga every time they saw a new type of seagull, all that really mattered was that we were having fun together.

Oh, Fang wants me to tell you that he saw a brown bear. Everyone got really excited about that, and the captain pulled the ship in close so everyone could get a picture of it. I made Fang stand at the rail with the bear behind him, and took a picture of him reaching out so it looks like he's petting the bear. It's a really cool picture.

I also took pictures of our cabin so you can see it when we get home, although there isn't much to see—there are two beds in an L shape, drawers under one bed, and a minuscule bathroom. That's pretty much it. Oh, and I know you—you probably want to know what happened with Fang and me sleeping together. Only we aren't really *sleeping* together; we just sleep *together*. . . . Oh, never mind, I'm not going to do that whole thing again. We turned the mattresses so our heads are next to each other, but that is as close as we can get. Bummer, huh?

Crap! I have to go again. Melba Toast has complained about me using the computer when it wasn't my turn, and Sam told me I have to get off. Back as soon as I can.

Hs & Ks
~Em

Subject: E & F: Tour—Day 3
From: emilyw@cruiseseattle.com
To: Dru@seattlegrrl.com
Date: July 7, 2005 11:12 pm

Where's that union place that fights for people's rights when you need them? The UFOCIO place, or whatever. I am being discriminated against because I'm younger than everyone here! The old people keep banding together to hog the computer. There's a notebook you're supposed to sign up in for time at the computer (the only one on board the ship), and every day when a new page is added for that day's time, the evil old ones get there before me and fill up the page. I sneaked on earlier today when someone didn't show up for her time, but Melba ratted on me and they made me get off while someone went and found the woman who was supposed to be on it. It's a conspiracy, I'm telling you! This is so illegal! I'm going to be writing to Amnesty International about this!

I'm not supposed to be on now, either, but there's a guy doing a talk about local Indians, and everyone is watching that, so I figured I could sneak out and use the 'puter now.

Siiiiiiiiiiiigh. Am. Being. Kicked. Off. Again . . .

~Em

Subject: Ship from Hell
From: emilyw@cruiseseattle.com
To: Dru@seattlegrrl.com
Date: July 9, 2005 5:54 am

They have banned me from the computer for the rest of the trip.

I am so going to be boycotting these cruise people!

~Em

Subject: Re: Sorry to worry you
From: Emster@seattlegrrl.com
To: Hollyberry@britsahoy.co.uk
Date: July 11, 2005 8:47 am

> *probably won't get this until you're back from your*
> *cruise, but I wanted to tell you that I'm fine, and no, I*
> *didn't cut myself. And thank you for worrying about*
> *me so much. Devon says you were really upset. I liked*
> *your tat story, too.*

Omigod! I have been *so worried* about you! Everyone has! Fang was worried, too! Even Mom asked whether you had been found. So you went to London? Why? I mean, I know it's cool and everything, and I like it there, but why did you go there? Did you go with Pearson?

I know family counseling sounds lamer than lame, but you know, it can't hurt you to go. Look at it this

169

way—it's the one time you can really complain about things and not have people tell you to get a grip and stuff like that. The therapist has to listen to you, because it's his job! So if I were you, I wouldn't clam up like you said you were going to—I'd let everyone know exactly what I was thinking and feeling. Otherwise, how will they know how to make things better for you?

> *I don't think a tattoo will make things better, though.*
> *It's not going to make Mum realize that I'm an adult*
> *now, and it won't make school more fun, and it cer-*
> *tainly won't get me a BF. Or do you think it will?*

You never know with tats! The very cool ones can work wonders!

And BTW, I never meant to say that you should get a tat. I just used the whole tat thing to show you what I did to help me get over my blues. You know, kind of motivational and all. It was just the right thing for me (and Brother) to do at the time. But you . . . well, you obviously need to do something different, especially since shooting off to London didn't seem to make things any better. I'll be happy to help you think of something that will help. Just let me know, and we'll hop into the Chat Girl chat room and do some serious Holly brainstorming, 'kay?

Subject: re: I'm back
From: Emster@seattlegrrl.com
To: Dru@seattlegrrl.com
Date: July 11, 2005 10:10 am

> *What do you mean, you got hypothermia in Alaska?*
> *It's summer! Who gets hypothermia in summer?*
> *What did you do to get banned from ever sailing on*
> *that cruise line again? And why was Fang arrested?*
> *Gah! I go away for a wedding (and you can be sure I*
> *will be taking notes, although we both know Debra*
> *has absolutely no taste), and you turn into the Amaz-*
> *ing Adventurous Emily! Tell everything! Thank heav-*
> *ens this hotel has Internet access. I'll check my e-mail*
> *as soon as I get back from the wedding, so SPILL*
> *NOW!*

Well, the Amazing Adventurous Emily is now the Amazing Emily with a Cold. It's the hypothermia, I think. Or just this curse thing that I'm sure is hanging over my head. If I wasn't sure there was a curse before, I know there is now, because only someone cursed could have the stuff happen to them that we had happen.

Oh, and by the way, say hi to your cousin for me. I don't remember a whole lot about her, except that she was a very cool babysitter, so do the congrats thing for me on getting married.

The cruise was OK until the second-to-the-last day. The first couple of days were pretty boring, except for the

Fang parts. It was really nice being able to just be with him. But then the birders found out he's almost a vet, and they sucked him into their group and made him talk about bird anatomy and stuff all day long, which, fortunately, he didn't mind (although let me tell you—there is nothing on this earth so dull as stuff about bird bones—I know that from waaaay too much experience!), although it cut a lot into our romantic alone-together time.

I told you this was a really small ship, right? It wasn't at all like a normal cruise ship. It was about a tenth of the size, holding only fifty people, which I thought at first was a rip because there was no pool, no casino, no shops except the gift counter in the lounge, and no fun events like shuffleboard contests and scavenger hunts (the old people killed that idea when it was suggested). There were bird lectures every night (which I ended up going to because Fang wanted to see them), and stuff about Alaska's history, which was meh, but even after they *cruelly* and *unfairly* banned me from using the computer, it was still an OK cruise. I read a lot, and Fang and I hung out together, and we ate tons and tons of food, and we watched sunsets and stuff, which was so romantic I wanted like mad to kiss him (but I couldn't, of course).

Anyhoo, everything was fine until the Day of Infamy.

"Em, come quick," Fang said on the fifth day as he burst into our cabin, where I was reading an Agatha Christie. "There's something you have to see."

"What?" I asked suspiciously, because I'm no fool. He'd dragged me out on deck to see ducks before. "Is it more ducks? Because we have ducks back home, you know. I can see lots and lots of ducks anytime I want."

"Those were extremely rare ducks," Fang said with a grin, his eyes twinkling. I had to admit that he seemed to be feeling much better ever since we'd gotten on the ship. He got his color back, and he said he wasn't feeling any more pains in his side, so that meant his spleen was shrinking back to normal size—yay! "But no, I swear there are no ducks."

"Not more icebergs? 'Cause I've seen enough of those, too. Not unless it's like *Titanic* icebergs and we're going to die or something."

"No, not more icebergs, although we are approaching the glacier, and I find the ice fields fascinating, but I won't make you look at any more of them. This is a waterfall. Come and see it."

"Oh," I said, picking up my book again. "We have waterfalls back home, too."

"Not like this," he said, taking the book and pulling me up by my good hand. He grabbed my jacket off the hook on the door and stuffed it on over my cast. "This waterfall has magical powers."

"Uh-huh," I said, allowing him to button me into my jacket because he was so excited, it made me go all woobidy in my knees. "Magical, eh?"

"Yes. Captain Jack said there's a legend that everyone who drinks from the falls will have his or her most heartfelt wish granted."

"Hmm," I said, kinda skeptical.

"And," he said, holding the door open for me, "it's supposed to favor lovers who are kept apart."

Now that had my attention. "Oooh! We're apart most of the time! We're not *lover* lovers, but we love each other, so that makes us kind of lovers, right?"

He just smiled and held up a coffee mug that he'd grabbed from the dining room. "Shall we?"

By the time we made it up to the bow (the pointy front part of the ship), the captain was pretty close to the waterfall. It looked just like every other waterfall—a bunch of water falling—but everyone was crammed into the bow clutching mugs, chatting about all the wishes they wanted granted.

Old people are pushy; let me just say that. I didn't even want to think about any of them falling into the lover category, so I didn't point out that they were way past being reunited with a parted lover, and just held Fang's hand while the captain nosed the bow of the ship to the very edge of the waterfall.

"Have at it, ladies and gents," Captain Jack called down from his ship-driving area at the top of the ship (it was called pilothouse or something silly like that). "Fortuna Falls! Good fortune will be sure to grace those who drink of her waters. Be quick, though. There's a wicked undercurrent that we're battling to stay in position, and I don't want to overheat the screws holding her in place." (I asked Fang later—*screws* have something to do with the engine of the ship.)

Now, here's where the curse part entered into it.

While everyone was having their turn holding out mugs and laughing and guzzling all the good-luck water, the ship was fine and dandy. But as soon as the crowd thinned out and Fang and I were just about to reach the rail, the captain called down that he was going to have to pull out because the current had become too strong.

"Hey!" I yelled, waving the mug up at the pilothouse. "We haven't had our water yet! And we're lovers who are parted most of the time, so we need it!"

"Sorry," Captain Jack yelled back at me, and started turning the ship. "We have to leave now. Stand away from the point of the bow. It will be a bit choppy as we back out."

"I've had it with being discriminated against," I told Fang. "I want some of that water, and dammit (sorry about the bad language, Dru, but I was really pissed), I'm going to have it! We need good luck!"

"Emily, you're not going to do what I think you're going to do—"

Fang didn't have time to finish before I threw myself onto the railing at the pointy part of the bow, leaning way out to shove my mug under the water.

"Emily, stop," Fang yelled, lunging for me.

"It's OK, I've got it," I said, hooking my cast around the railing to hold me in case I started to fall.

Captain Jack picked that moment to push the reverse button, or whatever you do to back a ship away from a waterfall, which, of course, meant I was suddenly leaning out into space with no ship beneath me. He bellowed something at me, and there was a horrible grinding noise as he evidently threw the ship forward again. The last thing I heard before I hit the water was him swearing at the top of his lungs when something at the back of the ship made a booming noise.

They fished me out of the waterfall. I heard later, when I was sitting in the first-aid cabin having a hot cup of tea as Sam the first mate cracked my cast off (it was soaked, so they figured they'd better take it off before it started to rot on my hand) that several of the evil ancients suggested just leaving me in the water, but Fang may have been joking about that. At least, I hope he was joking about it.

And don't let anyone tell you that the water in Alaska is anything but freezing, 'cause I'm here to tell you that there is a reason there are icebergs floating around there!

Sam and Polly made a fuss about warming up my core body temperature, wrapping me in a couple of electric blankies and making sure I could feel my toes and stuff, which I thought was nice until Sam finally got the cast off my hand.

"That doesn't look too bad," he said, gently brushing a bit of dusty stuff off the top of my hand. He turned it over and I screamed. The whole, entire bottom of my hand, my palm and all my fingers, was black. *Black*!

"Omigod, I have gangrene!" I screamed, my stomach doing a horrible clenching thing. "They're going to have to amputate it!"

"Em," Fang said from where he was standing behind me.

"Don't let them cut off my hand!" I yelled at him, snatching my hand back from Sam.

"Emily, it's not gangrene," Sam said. Fang put both his hands on my shoulders to keep me sitting down.

"Em, calm down," Fang said. "It's not gangrene. It's just blood."

"Eeeeeeeeeeeeeeeeek!" I screeched, flinging myself onto Fang. "Blood poisoning! I've got blood poisoning! I don't want to have my hand cut off!"

Yeah, OK, so I was overreacting just a tad, but you try being fished out of iceberg water and see how lucid you are. Especially if the whole underside of your hand is pitch-black.

"Em, it's just blood that collected when you broke your fingers. It's like a really deep bruise, nothing more. It will disperse with time. See? Look here—you can see it starting to fade on the edges." Fang stroked the side of my hand with one finger. "See the yellow? That's where the blood has been absorbed."

"It is?" I asked, clinging to hope.

"Yes. So stop freaking out, and let Sam put a splint on your hand."

"OK," I said, but I watched Sam carefully, just in case he got any ideas. I went to bed right after that (I think Sam had given me something to make me sleep when he had me drink some nasty-flavored tea), and pretty much was out of it for the rest of the day.

Captain Jack came in just as I was hobbling off to our cabin to go to sleep, and yelled at me for ignoring him when he told me to get away from the bow, telling me I had caused the engine to burn out some important thing that was going to cost a lot of money to fix, and warning me that if I did anything else to cause trouble, he'd have me put off the ship. I didn't get too worried about it, though—but that could be because I was almost asleep. Besides, the trip was almost over. And the following day was the day I'd been looking forward to the whole trip—glacier day!

We were supposed to hit the Samson Glacier (named for a guy who was killed trying to measure it) that night, but because of the broken-engine thing, it took us until the following morning to make it there. I'd heard that some guy who was a glacier expert was going to come onto the ship and talk about it before we did the trip out to see it in little boats.

"This is so exciting," I said to Fang as we pulled on our special glacier-walking boots. "This is worth falling in the water and having a gangrene hand!"

I didn't wait for Fang to tell me I didn't have gangrene (I knew that, but it was still freaky-looking), racing out of the cabin so I could check out the glacier before running into the lounge to save us good seats at the glacier guy's talk.

I'm here to tell you that glaciers are big. Really, really big. Well, maybe not all of them, but our glacier was big. Captain Jack said that legally the ship had to stay a quarter of a mile away from the iceberg in case it "spawned" (bits of it fell off into the water), but smaller expedition ships were allowed to zoom up close to it.

The glacier guy turned out to be a woman—Ranger Kristina—who was pretty cool. She had on glacier boots just like mine and Fang's, and did a slide show for about an hour telling us all about glaciers, how they moved, how they were constantly breaking up and reforming, yadda, yadda. It got a bit dull at the end, but I stuck it out because I wanted to be able to go check out the glacier, and you had to sit through her talk in order to do it.

"Right, who's for a little trip to see Samson up close and personal?" Ranger Kristina asked. Fang and I raised our hands immediately. There was a low mumbling sound behind us, and only my archenemies—Vern and Melba—decided to go with us.

"Excellent! Come with me, and we'll get you suited up. Everyone needs hats, gloves, and goggles!"

Yeah. Goggles. Bleah. Fang took a picture of me wearing my glacier wear, but no other living, breathing human being will ever see me with a goofy pom-pom hat, big furry gloves, and goggles on, so don't even ask.

We all climbed into Ranger Kristina's boat, which had big pontoon thingies on the sides (it looked very Jacques Cousteau), and off we zipped around the north side of the glacier.

"We're going to the north face because that's the side with land under it," RK yelled over the sound of the engine. "If the glacier were free-floating, we wouldn't be allowed to step foot on it. As it is, anything behind the two hundred-foot point is off-limits, since that part of the glacier is off the shore. It is against the law to go beyond that point, and park rangers such as myself have been deputized to arrest anyone who violates that law. In addition, the Parks Department has an agreement with the cruise ship operators; thus anyone violating the law will cause in a heavy fine for the cruise line, so be sure not to go beyond the warning markers."

I looked at the glacier as we zoomed by it. It was huge, really tall, like a couple of stories tall on the water side. A bunch of sea lions were lying around one edge of it, mostly males, RK said. The females and cubs were located closer to land, where there was more protection for the babies.

It took almost an hour to get to the land side, where a tiny little dock had been built so people could get out and climb onto the glacier. RK was right—just beyond the edge of the dock, on a low shelf of ice at the fringe of the glacier, a handful of sea lions were lounging around doing whatever sea lions do when they lie around on ice. I'd say sunbathe, except it was cloudy. There were also a few on the icebergs floating next to the glacier—Ranger Kristina said the icebergs were "children" of the glacier.

"Everyone stay together," she said as we tromped up

a narrow snowy path that led up from the dock. "Ah, it looks like we have the glacier to ourselves today. Excellent. If you follow those markers, you'll be taken to a good vantage point where you can see the whole of the bay."

"Oooh, Vern, let's get a picture of us with the bay behind," Melba said, grabbing Vern and dragging him off to where RK had pointed. Fang and I started out for the other side, so we could peek at the sea lions, but stopped when Melba screamed.

"What's wrong?" Fang asked as we ran back to where RK was squatting next to Vern, who was sitting on the ground.

"He twisted his leg in a hole. I don't think it's bad, but he should go back for some first aid treatment," RK said as she and Fang helped Vern onto his feet. "I'm sorry, but you'll have to come with us."

"What?" I said, waving my good hand around. "We just got here! We have special glacier boots and everything!"

"I know, and I'm sorry, but it's park policy to not allow unescorted guests to remain on the glacier."

"We won't hurt it," I said quickly, smiling my most trustworthy smile. "And we'll stay right here, behind the marker thingies, and we won't fall and hurt ourselves or anything."

"Well . . ."

Fang smiled. Amazingly, that was all it took.

"I'll be back as soon as I can to pick you up," RK said

as she slung an arm around Vern. "It won't be longer than an hour and a half. If you get cold, there's a shelter just beyond that ring of trees. There is wood for a fire, and emergency supplies if you get hungry or thirsty."

"Yay!" I said once they were out of earshot. "We have the glacier to ourselves! This is *so romantic!*"

Fang laughed. "Only you could find being stranded on an inhospitable, uninhabited two-mile-wide block of ice romantic, Em."

"Anywhere I'm with you is romantic," I said, fluttering my lashes at him.

"Now *that* is melty," he said, kissing my cheek before turning to examine the glacier. "Where do you want to look first?"

"Well, I want to go to the edge and watch bits of it break off, but I know you won't let me do that."

"Absolutely not," Fang said in a firm, Fangy sort of voice.

"You know, you can be a poop sometimes," I told him as we went to look at the baby sea lions. "Mr. Follows All the Laws."

"It keeps me out of trouble," he said complacently.

"Bah. Trouble. Sometimes you have to break the rules, you know?"

"I know. And I would have no problem breaking a law if it was for a good reason, but thus far I haven't had a good reason. Besides, keeping you out of trouble has become a little hobby of mine—which is becoming increasingly difficult when you insist on doing idiotic things despite warnings."

"I admitted that maybe it wasn't the smartest thing in the world to go after that waterfall water, but everything turned out OK. God knows I swallowed enough of it while I was waiting for Captain Jack to come back for me, so at least we'll have that good luck going for us. Oooh! Baby sea lions! Cute! Pictures!"

We stood at the edge of a steep icy slope down to the sea lion area (which was beyond the two hundred-foot markers, just my luck!) and looked at them for a bit. There were seven mom sea lions, and about six or seven babies. They all kind of lolled around on the ice, occasionally flapping a flipper like they were bored. I pulled out my digital camera and started taking pictures of them, but stopped when I zoomed in to get a good head shot of one of the babies.

"Fang!"

"What? I think that one going into the water is a bit older than the others. He's bigger than the rest."

"Look at the one sitting by itself—there's something around his neck. You can see it with the zoom."

Fang took the camera and looked where I was pointing. He swore (something you know he doesn't do very often). "Bloody hell. Looks like some plastic fishing line wrapped around his neck."

"He's bleeding," I said, holding my head next to

Fang's so I could look at the zoom screen with him. "It's cutting into his skin!"

"Yeah. I've seen pictures of otters with fishing line wrapped around them. It slowly strangles them unless it's removed."

"But that's just a baby!"

"Em—"

"A cute baby! Look at him! Look at that little furry face!"

"Even if I thought I could get the fishing wire off him, he's in the restricted area."

"You have to save it," I said, ducking down under the orange plastic ribbon thingie that marked off the edge of the safe zone. "I'll help. Come on!"

"Emily!"

I stopped and turned back to Fang. "You said you'd break a law if it was important."

"Yes, but—"

"You're almost a vet. Don't you have a moral obligation to try to help all animals?"

"And I want to help that sea lion, but—"

"That," I said, pointing dramatically down the slope, "is an animal in need! It's just a baby! And it's *bleeding*, Fang!"

"Oh, hell," he said, shoving my camera in his jacket pocket as he ducked under the tape. "If you say one word to anyone about this—"

"Not me," I said, doing the lips-zipped thing. "They can pull out my fingers, and I wouldn't breathe a word."

"Right, then. Do exactly as I say."

"You got it. I'm your helper girl."

"Stay behind me, keep your voice down, and move slow. Those females may look like they can't move fast, but if they think one of their pups is in danger, they won't balk at hurting us."

You can just stop making that face that I know you're making, Dru, because I did do exactly what Fang said. The closer we got to those sea lions—it's amazing how big they become up close—the more I realized that what he was going to do could possibly be dangerous for him.

"Be careful of your spleen," I warned as we slowly crept up to where the hurt baby was slumped up against an outcropping of ice. Fortunately all the other sea lions were clustered at the opposite end. A couple of the moms lifted their heads to look at us as we half walked, half slipped our way down the path, but no one came charging at us. The baby sea lion didn't do anything but make a couple of pathetic whimpers as Fang slowly squatted next to him.

"This is worse than I thought," Fang said softly as he slid his hand along the ground toward the pup. It flapped its flippers around a bit like it didn't like him, but I could see it was pretty sick. "The wound from the fishing line is badly infected. He needs antibiotics."

"Can you get the fishing line off him?" I asked, wiping back a couple of frosty tears. (That poor baby!)

"Not without surgery. It's gone too deep in his flesh. We have to get him medical care."

"OK," I said, pulling off my jacket. And you mocked me for getting the one with the thermal shell liner! I pulled out the shell and put the jacket back on. "Let's wrap him up in this, and then we can carry him back to Kristina when she comes. She can take us to the nearest vet's office."

"She's not going to like it," Fang said, edging my coat's shell around the baby. It was so sick it didn't even move.

"Big hairy deal. She can yell at me all she wants—I'm not going to leave that poor little baby sea lion there to die."

Fang flashed me a grin. "And you wonder why I love you."

"Eh," I said, standing up when he slowly got to his feet, the baby in his arms. "I never wondered about that. You're a smart man. You knew I was perfect for you."

"Something I knew right away, but it took you almost a year to realize it."

I made a face at him.

"Well, Miss Perfect, let's hope the pup's mother has abandoned him."

"Wouldn't it be better if she hadn't?" I asked. Fang took a step toward the path that led back to the safe zone, watching the sea lions. They didn't seem to give a hoot about us.

"Normally, yes, but in this case I'd rather not have to explain to an irate mother why I'm taking her pup away."

Just so you don't worry, we made it back to the top of the glacier without any of the sea lions doing anything to stop us from taking away the baby. A couple of them looked suspiciously at us, and one made noises that were probably sea lion swearing when I slipped on the path and knocked a bunch of snow on them, but we made it to the top just fine.

Just in time to be arrested. Well . . . Fang was, because he was holding the baby sea lion.

"Um, hi," I said to the guy in a brown parka with a ranger emblem on the front. He stood with his hands on his hips, glaring first at us, then behind him to where the don't-go-beyond-this-point tape was. A couple of tourists were behind the tape, taking pictures of stuff. "You must be another ranger guy bringing in people to see the glacier. We're here with Kristina. Only she had to run someone back to our ship. Ehm . . . I know this looks bad, but we can explain."

"Can you?" the man said. Then he got a whole lot glarier when the baby sea lion that was wrapped up in my jacket shell kicked its feet around. "And just what do you have there?"

"It's a juvenile sea lion pup that has been injured," Fang said, lifting the shell a little so the ranger could see. "I'm hoping we can transport him to the nearest vet facility."

"According to the Marine Mammal Protection Act of 1972, it is illegal for unauthorized persons to feed, handle, or harass all marine animals, including whales, dolphins, porpoises, dugongs, manatees, sea otters, polar bears, seals . . . and sea lions."

"Well, you see—" I started to say.

"This animal is gravely injured and could well die if it is not treated immediately," Fang said.

"The U.S. Fish and Wildlife Service is dedicated to preserving the safety of all marine mammals, and will prosecute to the fullest extent those who violate the law," the ranger said, totally ignoring us.

"Yeah, but—"

"I am aware that moving this animal is considered against the law," Fang said calmly, and I gave him a really bright smile for standing up to the ranger guy when all I wanted to do was yell at him. "But it violates my code of ethics to leave it when I can help it. You can arrest me if you like, but I'm going to see this injured pup to an authorized rescue facility or vet."

The ranger guy sneered. "Who do you think you are? You're not going to do anything other than put that animal back where you found it, then be taken into custody for violation of the Marine Mammal Protection Act."

Now, you know me, Dru. No one messes with cute little animals or my boyfriend while I'm around!

"You know what? I think you're in violation of that same law," I told the ranger guy. He tried to grab the sea lion from Fang, but Fang backed up, holding tight to it. "You're harassing that poor little injured baby worse than Fang is! All he wants to do is help it, and you want to put it back so it will die. Horribly! It's bleeding!"

"I am not authorized to rescue marine mammals any more than he is," the ranger said, trying to get around me to Fang. I blocked him. "What is wrong with you people? There are laws! There are specific rules to follow when an injured mammal is found. I intend to follow those rules. Now either put that animal back or give it to me."

"Rules? What rules? That little baby is going to die if he's not operated on *right now!* Do you want to have a baby sea lion death on your conscience?"

The ranger just looked at me. I decided I hated him. "I am just following the rules, ma'am. Now step out of the way."

What worked once could work again, I figured. I turned to the *touristas,* who were now clustered around the nearest point of the safe area, watching us. "Hey! This man wants to leave this innocent baby sea lion to die! My boyfriend is almost a vet! He's trying to get it some help! Would all of you mind taking pictures documenting how this horrible, vicious man is making my boyfriend—a man who has dedicated his life to protecting the health and welfare of innocent animals just like this sweet little baby sea lion—how he is making him leave this poor creature to die a cruel, lonely, painful, and totally unnecessary death?"

Three of the four people lifted their cameras and snapped pictures of Fang and the ranger.

"Now, hold on here," Ranger Dick said. "There are laws—"

"I plan on sending the photos to every newspaper and animal-rights group available to show how this man is abusing his power! Not to mention being personally responsible for the death of a baby sea lion!"

A man and a woman who were in matching bright red parkas gasped and looked outraged.

"It's not like that," the ranger said.

"Who is with me on seeing to it that people like him aren't allowed to hurt or kill any more innocent animals?" I yelled.

"We are!" the red jackets answered, both of them taking pictures as the ranger started toward me.

"How badly is the sea lion injured?" another man asked.

Fang carefully walked forward, peeling back the shell so they could see. All four people made horrified noises. "By my best estimate, this pup will die if it doesn't receive treatment in the next hour. It's unresponsive now, and does not have the strength or reserves necessary to survive without help much longer."

"I hope you all don't mind testifying that he"—I pointed to the ranger—"caused the baby's death by negligence!"

"I am not responsible for that animal's injuries," the ranger protested, and I knew I had him. (Maybe I should do law instead of physics? Naw. Physics is much more fun.)

"No, but you will be responsible for its death, which you could have averted," I said loudly, to make sure everyone heard. The red couple were making notes.

"Let's all be sure to get his name and his boss's name, so we can complain to everyone about a ranger that doesn't protect the animals he's supposed to be taking care of! I just bet there'll be a big, huge investigation!"

"But the rules say—"

"You have a choice," Fang interrupted, his eyes all cold and hard. I wanted to kiss him. Well, OK, I always want to kiss him, but I wanted to kiss him even more right then, when he was standing up to the bully ranger. "You can either follow your precious bloody rules, or you can save this animal's life. Which is it going to be?"

The ranger looked from the sea lion to Fang to the tourists, who stood with their cameras poised.

An hour later Ranger Kristina arrived at the glacier, and looked surprised to see me with four extra people. "Er . . ." she said.

"It's a long story," I said as we all trotted over to where she had pulled her expedition boat into the tiny dock. "This is Carol and Kim, and that's Henry, and that's Matte. He's Swedish. They're from Sunrise Cruises. Would you mind dropping them off at their ship?"

"How did they get here?" RK asked, looking around the glacier, but it was empty of everyone but us. "Where is the other ranger I saw heading this way?"

"He arrested Fang." RK's jaw dropped. I hurried to re-assure her. "Oh, it's OK, because he took Fang and the sea lion pup to some mammal rescue center. Fang said he would have someone on our ship notified about what happened to the baby, and I'm going to meet him tomorrow in Juneau. So everything is hunky dory, unless the baby was sicker than he thought, but you know, Fang is a really, really good almost-vet. He has an empathy for animals. So I trust him when he says he thinks the baby will pull through."

RK looked a little dazed by my explanation (I don't know why—it makes perfect sense to me), but in the end she took us back to our ships. The only thing is, when I told her what happened, she yelled at me for going beyond the safe zone.

Captain Jack yelled at me as well.

"You're a troublemaker," he said, pointing his finger at me. "Not only are you directly responsible for the damage to the ship's engine; now I have to pay a two-thousand-dollar fine for your violation of park limits!"

"I said I was sorry about the ship thingie, but it's totally unfair of Kristina to pick on me for helping to rescue a hurt baby sea lion," I argued, but it was no use.

Captain Jack took a couple of deep breaths and finally said, "You are banned from ever sailing on my ship again," before turning around and marching away.

I pretty much stayed in my cabin the rest of the day. For one thing we were arriving in Juneau the next morning, and I had to get my things as well as Fang's packed up. But mostly I stayed there because all the bird oldsters looked at me like I had killed Fang or something.

"Had him arrested," I caught one of them muttering as I headed in for dinner.

"She has no interest in birds, none whatsoever. I just can't trust someone who doesn't like birds," another one answered.

"Don't forget she tried to make us believe she was married to him," Melba said, making mean eyes at me. "As if that nice Fang would marry such a jade!"

I ignored them all, which wasn't too hard, since they ignored me as well. Unfortunately, it was supposed to be our table's turn to have the captain eat with us (I don't know why this was supposed to be such a big deal, but everyone had been excited about it). Captain Jack walked in, saw that the only empty seat was next to me, and said really loudly, "I've lost my appetite."

So that's it. That was our cruise. The flight home was uneventful, thank God. They ended up dropping the charges against Fang, but only after he got the British Consul in Anchorage involved. It helped that the rescue center where Fang and the ranger (I never did find out his name) went praised Fang up one side and down the other for his quick actions in saving the baby sea lion.

I'm pooped. Today was the deadline for picking a dorm or student house, and I decided that although a dorm might be have more freedom, I'd go ahead and try one of the student houses. There's a science house for students of astronomy, physics, and engineering, so I applied to it. I saw some of the students hanging around the physics building—they're geeky, but tolerable. They need some serious fashion tips, though (I'm so going to have my work cut out for me there!) Fingers crossed I get it! Everyone there gets their own room, but I'd have to have a roomie in a dorm. I wouldn't mind a roomie so much, but what happens if Dermott comes with me? How on earth am I going to explain an underwear drawer ghost to someone? Gah!

Maybe Dermott is part of the curse on me? Hmm. Must go Google ghosts and curses.

Hugs and all that,
~Em

Subject: re: No one understands!
From: Emster@seattlegrrl.com
To: Hollyberry@britsahoy.co.uk
Date: July 14, 2005 10:10 am

> *but I don't feel depressed! Depressed people try to*
> *kill themselves, and look horrible, and turn into street*
> *people and things. I'm not doing any of that! I just*
> *want everyone to leave me alone.*

Well, I'm no expert on depression or anything, but I did go through that whole leading-up-to-the-tat thing, and if that wasn't depressing, I don't know what was.

So I'm gonna go out on a limb here, Hol, and say that maybe this doctor isn't so far off base as you think (All Your Base Are Belong To Us! Heh heh heh. Sorry. Just wanted to make you smile).

> *You said you thought you were cursed, but I know I*
> *am. I don't have a SP, school is horrible, my family*
> *hates me, and you're on the other side of the world.*
> *Sniff.*

You may not have a snogging partner (hee . . . SP, cute!), but you have LOADS of friends who care about you, including me and Dru and Fang. Long distance care is almost as good as local care, and for that, I've authorized Devon to go around and bother you whenever you need bothering.

> *Dr. Eccles wants me to take antidepressants. You*
> *know how I feel about drugs!*

Yeah, but these are drugs that'll help you feel better. I'm totally with you on the whole drug thing—I only take ibu when the cramps get really bad—but sometimes, Holly, you have to take some meds to get better. I took pain meds for my broken hand, and it helped. Fang took antibiotics for his streph throat, and it went away really fast. So maybe if you take these antidepressants for a bit, and do that counseling thing he wants you to do with your fam, then things'll get better for you.

They can't possibly get any worse, can they?

Big, big smoochies, and oodles of hugsies to let you know I miss you, and I'm here for you when you want to vent,

~Em

EYELINER OF THE GODS
KATIE MAXWELL

To Whom It May Concern:

If you find this letter, it means that I, January James, have fallen down the burial shaft of the Tomb of Tekhen and Tekhnet where I'm spending a month working as a conservator, and am probably lying at the bottom, dead from a broken leg and thirst. . . .

To whoever finds my sand-scoured, withered corpse:

I'm dead. It's the mummy's curse. Don't blame Seth, he was just trying to help, even if everyone does say he's the reincarnation of an evil Egyptian god. He's not. I know, because no one who kisses like he does can be truly evil.

Help! I'm stuck in Egypt with a pushy girl named Chloe, a cursed bracelet, and a hottie who makes my toes curl. . . .

Dorchester Publishing Co., Inc.
P.O. Box 6640
Wayne, PA 19087-8640

5378-0
$5.99 US/$7.99 CAN

Please add $2.50 for shipping and handling for the first book and $.75 for each additional book. NY and PA residents, add appropriate sales tax. No cash, stamps, or CODs. Canadian orders require an extra $2.00 for shipping and handling and must be paid in U.S. dollars. Prices and availability subject to change. **Payment must accompany all orders.**

Name: _____

Address: _____

City: _____ State: _____ Zip: _____

E-mail: _____

I have enclosed $_____ in payment for the checked book(s).

CHECK OUT OUR WEBSITE! www.smoochya.com
_____ *Please send me a free catalog.*

What's French For "EW!"?

KATIE MAXWELL

Subject: Emily's Handy Phrases For Spring Break in Paris
From: Em-the-enforcer@englandrocks.com
To: Dru@seattlegrrl.com

J'apprendrais par coeur plutôt le Klingon qu'essaye d'apprendre le français en deux semaines.
I would rather memorize Klingon than try to learn French in two weeks.

Vous voulez que je mange un escargot?
You want me to *EAT* a snail?!?

Vous êtes nummy, mais mon petit ami est le roi des hotties, et il vient à Paris seulement pour me voir!
You are nummy, but my boyfriend is the king of hotties, and he's coming to Paris just to see me!

Dorchester Publishing Co., Inc.
P.O. Box 6640
Wayne, PA 19087-8640

5297-0
$5.99 US/$7.99 CAN

Please add $2.50 for shipping and handling for the first book and $.75 for each additional book. NY and PA residents, add appropriate sales tax. No cash, stamps, or CODs. Canadian orders require an extra $2.00 for shipping and handling and must be paid in U.S. dollars. Prices and availability subject to change. **Payment must accompany all orders.**

Name: _____
Address: _____
City: _____ State: _____ Zip: _____
E-mail: _____

CHECK OUT OUR WEBSITE! www.smoochya.com
_____ Please send me a free catalog.

They Wear WHAT Under Their Kilts?
by Katie Maxwell

Subject: Emily's Glossary for People Who Haven't Been to Scotland
From: Mrs.Legolas@kiltnet.com
To: Dru@seattlegrrl.com

Faffing about: running around doing nothing. In other words, spending a month supposedly doing work experience on a Scottish sheep farm, but really spending days on Kilt Watch at the nearest castle.

Schottie: Scottish Hottie, also known as Ruaraidh.

Mad schnoogles: the British way of saying big smoochy kisses. Will admit it sounds v. smart to say it that way.

Bunch of yobbos: a group of mindless idiots. In Scotland, can also mean sheep.

Stooshie: uproar, as in, "If Holly thinks she can take Ruaraidh from me without causing a stooshie, she's out of her mind!"

Sheep dip: not an appetizer.

Dorchester Publishing Co., Inc.
P.O. Box 6640 _____5258-X
Wayne, PA 19087-8640 $5.99 US/$7.99 CAN

Please add $2.50 for shipping and handling for the first book and $.75 for each additional book. NY and PA residents, add appropriate sales tax. No cash, stamps, or CODs. Canadian orders require $2.00 for shipping and handling and must be paid in U.S. dollars. Prices and availability subject to change. **Payment must accompany all orders.**

Name: _____
Address: _____
City: _____ State: _____ Zip: _____
E-mail: _____

***CHECK OUT OUR WEBSITE!* www.smoochya.com**
_____ *Please send me a free catalog.*

Didn't want this book to end?

There's more waiting at **www.smoochya.com**:

Win FREE books and makeup!
Read excerpts from other books!
Chat with the authors!
Horoscopes!
Quizzes!

 smooch Bringing you the books on everyone's lips!